THE EERIE ECHO

THE EERIE ECHO

REBECCA PRICE JANNEY

WORD PUBLISHING
Dallas • London • Vancouver • Melbourne

THE EERIE ECHO

Copyright © 1993 by Rebecca Price Janney.

Managing Editor: Laura Minchew
Project Editor: Beverly Phillips

Library of Congress Cataloging–in–Publication Data

Janney, Rebecca Price, 1957–
    The eerie echo / Rebecca Price Janney.
        p.   cm.—(The Heather Reed mystery series ; #3)
    "Word kids!"
    Summary: On Professor Samra's student tour to Israel, Heather and
the sixteen-year-old son of a British diplomat are caught up in a menacing
duo's search for a priceless religious treasure.
    ISBN 0–8499–3400–1
    [1. Mystery and detective stories.] I. Title. II. Series : Janney,
Rebecca Price, 1957–   Heather Reed mystery series ; #3.
PZ7.J2433Ee   1993
[Fic]—dc20   92–45711
                                                                          CIP
                                                                          AC

Printed in the United States of America

3 4 5 6 7 8 9 LBM 9 8 7 6 5 4 3 2 1

For Sylvia Eagono, Glenn Long, Conny Mus,
Bert and Barbara Freeston, and Florence Murphy:
"There is a friend who sticks closer than a brother."

Contents

1

Cry from a Holy Cave

I can't believe it—Bethlehem in the snow!" Heather Reed exclaimed.

"It's amazing," her brother Brian agreed.

She tapped the bus driver on the back. "Does it snow here like this very often?"

"I have seen it only twice," he answered.

"When?" the sixteen-year-old pursued.

"Yesterday and today."

Several students in the front laughed at his remark. As the vehicle made its way toward the ancient town of Bethlehem, Dr. George Samra picked up the bus's microphone. The famous history professor was leading a group of Kirby College students on a tour of Israel.

Brian Reed attended Kirby and came on the trip with his roommate, Joe Rutli. Heather, a high-school junior, had been allowed to go because of her excellent grades and her friendship with Dr. Samra.

"Just don't expect me to keep her out of trouble," Brian had informed their parents. Heather often got into mischief, but she was also good at solving mysteries. In her last case, A MODEL MYSTERY, she kept a beauty contest from turning into a deadly disaster.

Dr. Samra addressed his students. "This snow was quite unexpected. I'm glad many of you took Dr. Coffey's advice and wrapped plastic bags around your footwear."

Heather glanced at her jogging shoes. She had slept so hard after the twelve-hour flight that she missed breakfast and the other professor's announcement about shoe protection. Dr. Cindy Coffey traveled widely as an art historian and had many tips to share.

"I read in today's paper that this is the heaviest snow the country has ever had," Dr. Samra continued. "You saw a rare sight last evening as we drove to our hotel— snow on the Dome of the Rock." He referred to the thirteen-hundred-year-old Moslem shrine. "No doubt you think of Bethlehem wrapped in snow because of Christmas cards. But this kind of weather is actually uncommon here. I hope you will all enjoy it. You can tell people you were in Israel at this exceptional time."

"I'll bet there's at least a foot of snow on the ground," Joe Rutli observed.

Heather turned sideways so she could talk to him and Brian. "I wonder if we'll see shepherds. The town seems too modern for them."

"After we visit the Church of the Nativity, we'll drive out to Shepherd's Field," Dr. Samra said from across the aisle. "I'm certain you will see some shepherds with their sheep there."

The bus came to a stop in Manger Square. It was almost deserted, except for some soldiers acting as guards. Then tall, slender Dr. Coffey spoke to the group of twenty. "As you can see, there aren't many tourists here today. Our bus driver says the snow is keeping people from getting out and about today, so we will have the church mostly to ourselves. When you leave the bus, walk through the courtyard to the entrance. But don't go inside until we are all together."

Heather eagerly grabbed her backpack and hopped off the bus, but she abruptly stopped in her tracks. "Oh yuk!" the teenager groaned, as thick snow mixed with water oozed into her sneakers. She stepped off to the side as the others sloshed their way through the cold slush.

"I have extra plastic bags at the hotel," Heather's roommate, Michelle Weston, told her. "I'm just sorry I didn't think of it before."

"Me, too," Heather sighed.

Michelle's boyfriend, Tito Catafino, walked over. "What a mess!" he exclaimed.

"I don't have any bags big enough for your feet," Michelle teased him.

About half the group did not have adequate shoes. They complained as they slogged through the snow to the church courtyard.

"The snow wasn't this yucky in Jerusalem," Brian observed.

Joe laughed. "It had been washed away with a water hose there."

"That's how it got so icy!" Heather stated.

Suddenly a group of street vendors swarmed around the American college students. A teenager about Heather's age waved postcards in her face. "One American dollar!" he shouted.

She remembered Dr. Coffey's advice concerning such merchants: If you don't want to buy anything, you should not look at them or their items. If you do, then bargain to get the best price.

As Heather trudged miserably through the cold, wet sludge, the hawker followed her closely. "One American dollar," he kept repeating. When she continued to show no interest, the young man went on to someone else. Then Heather felt a strong hand support her right elbow.

"I'd hate to see you fall in this mess," Brian said.

His sister's hazel eyes sparkled in the morning sun. "You're a real pal. Thanks."

The group paused outside the unusually small door to the large, impressive church. Dr. Coffey joked, "You may wonder whether people were shorter back then. Actually, the entrance is tiny for a much different reason. Centuries ago the opening was quite large. But invaders rode on horseback right through it into the church.

So the priests lowered the doorway for protection. Be sure to watch your heads as we go inside."

The Americans bent low to get through and found themselves in an enormous area. "It seems huge after that door," Heather whispered to Joe.

She had never seen such a massive church. But there were, oddly, no pews. Professor Coffey said that there were actually three churches on the site and that two of them had no seats. The professor led them to a large opening in the floor. Heather's teeth chattered in the damp chill. *This isn't exactly inspiring,* she thought. She couldn't imagine attending a service there.

"Notice this cut-away portion of the floor," said Dr. Coffey. The students huddled around it, quietly stomping their feet to get warm. "The mosaic underneath is part of the floor of the original church," she explained. "Do any of you recall the name of the first Roman emperor who became a Christian?"

"Constantine," they said in unison.

"Very good," she praised. "His mother Helena came here in the fourth century and learned Jesus was born here. So Constantine built the church, and it is among the oldest in the world." Then she pointed to a spot across the room. "Let's go to that marble archway. It leads down to the site where tradition says Jesus was actually born."

Heather eagerly followed the woman to a beautiful marble arch flanked by crimson and gold curtains. But a pained cry from the cave below tore through the solemn atmosphere. Instinctively Heather raced down the steps to find out what was going on.

2

Panic in Manger Square

"Don't go down there!" Dr. Coffey yelled.

But it was too late. Heather was already at the bottom of the steps, where she spotted a man fleeing through another door. Then she noticed the screamer—a distressed priest. He shouted something Heather couldn't understand, then pointed frantically at the escaping figure. She ran through a second door after the man. On the other side, Heather saw another church sanctuary. The man raced through it as different priests watched in annoyance.

Heather didn't know where she was going. She simply followed the fleeing figure. *Maybe he's from around here,* she considered briefly. Then she changed her mind. Although she was too far from the man to see his face, Heather noted he was tall. She also saw that his hair was short, grayish-brown, and his skin was fairly light in color. Most of the locals, however, were short, dark-haired, and had olive-skinned complexions. The young detective also noticed that the man was clutching a crowbar in one hand. *He must have robbed or tried to rob the church,* she guessed.

As he darted out to the courtyard, Heather sighed. *More slush,* she thought grimly. The man must have been wearing weatherproof shoes because he passed through the snow effortlessly.

As the teenager struggled to keep the man in sight, she saw something drop out of his coat pocket. She made a mental note of where the object fell so she could go back for it later.

The man turned around briefly to see who was chasing him. And in that instant, Heather was able to see that he was rather stern-looking and middle-aged. He grinned smugly.

I'm never going to catch him now, the teenager thought.

Then just as she was giving up the chase, Heather saw the two soldiers she'd noticed earlier in Manger Square. *Too bad they weren't closer to the church,* she thought. *Then they would have seen the thief, and me chasing him.* "Excuse me!" Heather called loudly. They eyed her curiously.

"*Boker tov,*" the shorter one said.

"What?" she asked, panting.

"Good morning," he said in heavily-accented English.

"Uh, *shalom,*" she said awkwardly. (*Shalom* meant "hello" in Hebrew.) "A man just tried to steal something from the church, and I can't catch him," she said rapidly, pointing in his direction.

The soldier's face went blank. Then he asked her something in Hebrew.

"I can't understand you," she said impatiently. The man was almost out of sight by now. "Don't you speak English?"

"A little," he said.

Heather grabbed the soldier's arm and turned him in the man's direction. "Bad man!" she yelled. "Bad man!"

Although she felt like an actress in an old movie about cowboys and Indians, the soldier's face lit up. He said something to his partner in Hebrew, and they took off after the guy. Heather stood there in her cold shoes feeling miserable. She waited for a few minutes, hoping the soldiers would return with the thief. When they did not, the girl wandered back toward the church.

On the way she looked for the item the man had dropped. Heather's efforts were quickly rewarded when she spotted it glistening in the sun. She picked it up and saw that it was a French coin. (Her French teacher would be proud of her for recognizing the language written on the shiny piece of money). She slipped it into her coat pocket.

Heather saw that the Kirby group had moved on to the second sanctuary. Although Brian was craning his neck to see where his sister had gone, she slipped by undetected, using the giant pillars for cover. She wanted to talk to the priest before rejoining them.

Near the stairs leading to the site of Christ's birth, Heather saw the priest. He quickly advanced in her direction.

"I'm afraid I didn't catch that man," she apologized.

"No?" he asked, cocking his head to one side. Heather saw that in spite of his very imposing black robe, he seemed quite young. "He got away?" His voice was accented but understandable.

"Yes," she admitted. "I'm very sorry."

"I am as well," he said sadly.

"What did he try to steal?" she inquired. When Heather shifted her weight, her left shoe made a loud squishy noise. She blushed, and the priest grinned in spite of himself.

"I went downstairs to light the lamps in the holy grotto when I saw the man trying to steal the star."

"The star?" Heather asked.

"Yes. On the site of our Lord's birth is a beautiful silver star. It is very sacred." He took her to the place and showed it to her. The star was beautifully crafted. "Another terrible offense," he said with a faraway look. But before Heather could ask what he meant, the priest said, "I frightened him with my cry, and he ran off."

"What did you mean by 'another offense?'" she interrupted.

"We attract evildoers," he mourned. But he would not explain.

"Did you get a good look at him?" Heather pursued.

"I was too astonished. But he was tall, and his hair was turning gray," he supplied.

"Um," she responded. "That's what I saw too. I chased him, but the snow slowed me down," Heather said.

"Then I found a couple of soldiers, and they went after him. I'm sure they'll let you know if they catch the guy." Then she pulled out the coin he dropped and showed it to the priest. "Does this mean anything to you?"

He turned it over a few times and shook his head. "I am sorry." He gave it back. "Perhaps this man is French?"

"That's what I think," she pursed her lips. "Well, Father, uh . . ."

"Dimitri," he supplied.

"Father Dimitri, I need to catch my group. They'll wonder what happened to me. If I learn anything else, I'll be sure to let you know."

"I appreciate your helpfulness," the priest thanked her. "I did not learn your name, and I should like to know it."

"Heather Reed."

"God bless you, Miss Reed," he said, bowing slightly. He made the sign of the cross over her, then Heather rejoined her group.

Dr. Samra caught her eye, and she quietly went over and told him what happened. Brian and Joe joined them. Heather was excited! She couldn't stop thinking about the possibility of having a mystery to solve in Israel.

"Heather, adventure seems to be your middle name!" the professor exclaimed. "But do be careful," he added. "Nasty things happen in this part of the world."

No one knew that better than Dr. Samra. In fact, it was his curious teenaged-friend here who had solved a dangerous mystery involving his disappearance after one of Samra's study trips in the Middle East.

Heather's brother angrily interrupted her conversation with the professor. "I will not have you spoil my trip," he insisted. "I'm here to learn. If you get involved in any crazy schemes, I'll call Mom and Dad, and they'll put a stop to it." His dark brown eyes flashed.

"Okay, okay," she said. But deep inside, Heather knew she couldn't resist a mystery any more than she could turn down a pizza bagel.

The soldiers hadn't returned when the American students climbed back into the bus. Heather felt frustrated not knowing whether or not they caught the thief. The teenager was, however, grateful for the warmth of the vehicle. Her feet were freezing.

On the way back to Jerusalem they stopped first at Shepherd's Field and then went to an olive-wood curio shop. A shivering Heather gratefully accepted a cup of hot tea from a clerk. "They should do this in America," she whispered to Michelle. She and Brian purchased a beautiful crèche for their parents.

Heather was even happier when they arrived at their unique hotel. The Kibbutz Yehuda was a farming community like others in Israel. Its members raised all their food and ran a hotel. Heather liked the comfortable room she shared with fun-loving Michelle Weston, but she was particularly glad to take a hot shower and change into dry clothes. The professors had encouraged the students to relax during the afternoon to overcome their jet lag.

That evening their tour group dined at a restaurant on the Mount of Olives where they had a breathtaking view of the Old City. Dominating the scene was the beautiful Dome of the Rock, its gold top covered with snow.

"Isn't that spectacular?" Heather asked her brother.

He agreed. "I've never seen anything like it before."

They enjoyed a marvelous roast beef dinner, then went to The Israeli Folklore Festival. "I heard this is a great show," Joe commented as he and Brian sat down on either side of Heather.

"I'm not too crazy about folk dancing," Brian said uncertainly.

"You may like this," Joe countered. "Dr. Samra has seen it before and says the costumes are terrific. Plus the emcee greets the audience in about twenty different languages."

"Well, I'll give it a try," said Brian, still not convinced.

Heather opened her program, but it slipped right out of her hand and went under the seat in front of her. The guy sitting there picked it up. When he turned around to hand it back to Heather, her eyes nearly popped out.

3

The Diplomat's Son

I believe you dropped this," said the cutest guy Heather had ever seen. He had a musical English accent and was close to Heather's age. His light brown hair, cut stylishly short, framed a square, intelligent face. He smiled and handed the program back to her.

"Thank you," she said shyly.

"Are you an American?" he asked. His warm, brown eyes sparkled under the house lights.

"Yes, I am," she answered. "My name is Heather Reed."

"And I'm Graham Ogden," he replied.

"Are you from Great Britain?"

He smiled again and nodded. "That's right. And you seem to be with a group."

"Yes, I am. We're from Kirby College in Pennsylvania. This is my brother, Brian, and his friend Joe Rutli. Guys, meet Graham Ogden."

The college students shook his hand, though it was awkward with the seats separating them.

"Are you in college?" Graham asked Heather.

"No," she laughed. "But a professor with us is a good friend, and since my brother goes there, they let me come on the study tour."

Joe cupped a hand against his mouth and whispered to Graham, "Don't let her kid you—she's brilliant!"

Heather's cheeks colored. Then a large, middle-aged man sat down next to Graham. She wondered if they were related, but she'd have to wait to find out because the curtain opened, and the orchestra began playing.

"I'll talk to you later," Graham said.

The vibrant emcee lived up to his reputation. He delighted the audience by greeting them in several different languages, as Joe had predicted.

"Good evening, British friends!" he greeted. "Did you have your spot of tea in your flat today? God save the Queen! Cheerio!"

Heather heard Graham laugh heartily. Then it was her turn when the master of ceremonies continued, "And to the Americans—hiya! How are ya! Baseball, hot dogs, and Mom's apple pie."

He made the welcome in fifteen different languages. Then the emcee introduced each folk dance in either Hebrew, Arabic, English, French, German or Spanish.

Heather thoroughly enjoyed the skilled performers as they did a variety of Jewish and Arab dances. Their traditional costumes were breathtaking. It was also a treat to watch Graham Ogden!

During the ten-minute intermission Heather got up to stretch. The man who had joined Graham spoke to him, and then both rose and turned toward Heather.

"Hi again," she said. "Isn't it a marvelous show!"

Graham nodded. "It is quite nice. I'm glad I came tonight."

Heather blushed again. She hoped Brian and Joe wouldn't tease her in front of Graham.

"Heather Reed, I'd like you to meet my father, Mr. Nigel Ogden."

He had remembered her name! Heather's heart fluttered oddly. "Hello, Mr. Ogden," she said, shaking the man's extended hand.

"It's a pleasure to meet you," he smiled. His English accent was also thick.

Nigel Ogden was well over six feet tall. His large build dwarfed his son's smaller frame. And although Graham's hair was light brown, his father's was blond and rather wind-blown. The older man's crystal blue eyes regarded Heather cordially. *Graham must look more like his mother*, she thought.

Introductions were made all around, and Dr. Samra came over to meet the friendly strangers. Heather thought she heard Mr. Ogden say something about the diplomatic corps. She wanted to ask about it, but the music started again, signaling people back to their seats.

After the delightful show, Heather reluctantly got up to leave. She was about to say good-bye to Graham when he totally surprised her.

"My father and I are going to a coffee shop. Would you like to join us?" His brown eyes wore a hopeful expression. "We'll drive you to your hotel afterward."

Heather wanted to go but didn't know if she could. "I'll ask Dr. Samra," she declared.

The pretty teenager scooted out of the row and found Dr. Samra talking with some students. She excused herself and asked his permission. To her surprise he granted it rather quickly. When she returned, Brian eyed her with some suspicion, but his roommate moved him along.

"Don't worry about Brian," Joe told Heather. "I'll deal with him."

"Dr. Samra said I could go," Heather reported to the Ogdens. "But I must be back by eleven-thirty."

"That gives us over an hour," Graham said brightly, directing Heather outside into the cold night air. Quickly, the three of them buttoned up their coats.

"We'll walk to the coffee shop," Mr. Ogden said. "It's only a block and a half away. We can leave the car here." Then he held onto Heather's arm. "Please be careful of the ice. Israelis are not used to coping with winter weather."

The coffee shop bustled with activity because many people had stopped there after the performance. The host recognized Mr. Ogden and gave them a nice table near a window. A waiter took their orders for coffee and nut pastries, then left.

"My son tells me you are from Pennsylvania," Mr. Ogden began. "I visited Philadelphia last year for a conference. How far from it are you?"

"About twenty miles," Heather said. "I live near Valley Forge. Have you heard of it?"

"Oh, yes," he said. Graham nodded as well.

"And you have a brother," Mr. Ogden said.

"That's right. It's just us and our parents." He seemed interested, so Heather told him, "My father is the managing editor of a Philadelphia paper. My mother's a pediatrician." A sad look briefly darkened Graham's face. Heather wondered what it meant. "Do you live in Jerusalem?"

"Yes," Graham answered. "My father is a British diplomat and has been here for two years. I've lived here for ten months."

Mr. Ogden explained, "Graham's mother died twelve years ago. Because of my constant travels, he lived with her parents."

"Oh, I see," Heather commented. "You seem happy to be together."

Her new friend grinned. "We are."

The waiter arrived with their coffee and pastries. They didn't speak again until he left.

Heather asked, "Do you like Jerusalem?"

"Oh, yes. It's very exciting," Graham replied.

"At times too exciting!" his father added.

"Do you think it's dangerous?" she asked.

"More than many places, yes," the diplomat answered. "But I personally have never been afraid." He took a big bite of pastry and a sip of coffee.

Heather tried her dessert and found it delicious. "This is fantastic!"

"I'm glad you like it," Graham commented. "I love their pastries here. They use nuts in many dishes in Israel."

"What is your college group studying?" Mr. Ogden asked.

"Jewish history," she explained.

"For how long will you be here?"

"Just two weeks," she replied. She was beginning to wish it were much longer.

"Can you use the credits when you get to college?" Graham inquired.

"Yes. That is, if I do well," she joked. "Where do you go to school, Graham?"

"At an English one for children of diplomats. I'm in my third year."

"I think that would be the junior class in America," his father explained.

"I'm in my junior year," Heather grinned.

"What themes do you like?" the teenager asked.

"Themes?" she was puzzled.

"Uh, subjects," Graham clarified.

"I like history," she said. "And English."

"Me, too," he agreed.

Mr. Ogden asked where she was staying.

"At the Kibbutz Yehuda. But we will also go on a three-day trip to Tiberias," she told the diplomat.

"That isn't much time," Graham remarked.

Heather shook her head and felt her long, honey-brown hair swish gently. "No, it isn't."

"Will you visit other places too?" he questioned.

"Yes. The Dead Sea and the caves there, the Sea of Galilee, and the Mediterranean coast."

"Will your professors lecture?" Mr. Ogden asked, forking his last piece of pastry.

"Yes. Dr. Samra teaches history, and Dr. Cindy Coffey lectures on art and architecture. We'll also hear guest speakers at Hebrew University."

"What a full schedule!" Mr. Ogden commented. "I hope you have a wonderful time."

"I already am! The snow itself is such a surprise." She grinned. "Except I didn't bring boots."

"It certainly has been unexpected," he agreed.

"Were you able to get about much today?" Graham asked.

"Yes, we have a very good bus driver." Heather suddenly thought about the incident at the Church of the Nativity. She decided to tell them about it. "A man tried to steal the star," she concluded. "I ran after him, but he got away. I did find this, though." She reached into her coat pocket and produced the French coin. "He dropped this in the courtyard."

Graham asked to see it. "Look Dad! It's French."

His father took the coin, and Heather watched a deep frown darken his normally friendly face.

4

Mystery and Romance

W hat's wrong?" Heather asked.

The British diplomat cleared his throat. Then he handed the coin back and leaned heavily into the chair. "There's great tension in this region," he said vaguely. "Anything can spark a deadly conflict. Especially something like this."

"I don't quite understand," the American teenager shook her head.

"You see, Heather, the Holy Places are protected by the Israeli government." He cleared his throat again. "The incident you witnessed could be explosive if not handled correctly."

"You mean church officials might blame the government for not protecting the building?"

"That's one possibility," he replied.

"Or maybe a misguided person or group might avenge the church by punishing a Frenchman?" Graham inquired.

His father nodded gravely. "A few weeks ago some masked terrorists threw stones and bottles at the soldiers guarding Manger Square. Several tourists got caught in the crossfire and were injured."

"How terrible!" Heather cried out.

"Perhaps you shouldn't tell anyone else about this coin," Mr. Ogden suggested. "My good friend works at the French Consulate. I'll talk to him about it." He handed the coin back to Heather.

"Okay. You *will* let me know if you discover something, won't you?" she asked. "I'm interested in this."

"Of course, the coin might not mean anything," he cautioned. "You don't have to be French to carry that country's currency," he observed.

Suddenly Heather had an unpleasant thought. What if Mr. Ogden knew something he couldn't—or wouldn't—pass along? She knew he couldn't have been the thief because Mr. Ogden was a lot bigger than the suspect. *But he might know the thief or what's going on,* she reflected.

"Just one more thing," she said. "Who would do such a cheeky thing?"

Mr. Ogden frowned, and his son giggled. "I think she means 'forward,'" Graham explained. He smiled at Heather, who looked embarrassed.

His father seemed uncomfortable continuing the discussion. "I really don't know who would want to steal the star," he said.

Graham looked excited about the mystery. "I think a thrill-seeker might have tried to take it. Or maybe a dishonest scholar."

"Someone who wanted a special souvenir?" Heather asked humorously.

"Exactly," he affirmed.

"Then again, it might have been the work of an emotionally misguided individual. Jerusalem attracts such people."

Mr. Ogden waved his hand as if to wipe their conversation clean. "We should take Heather back to the kibbutz, Graham. It is getting late."

The discussion about the star ended. The British diplomat paid the bill, and they carefully made their way across the ice to his worn-looking vehicle.

When they pulled up to the kibbutz hotel entrance, Heather thanked them for a fun evening.

"I enjoyed meeting you," she said politely.

Mr. Ogden seemed like his cheerful self again. "It was our pleasure," he returned. "I hope we see you again." His clear blue eyes twinkled mischievously.

"I'll walk Heather to the door," Graham announced.

"Tonight was such fun," Heather told him. Then an unwelcome yawn escaped, and they both laughed. "Please excuse me! Believe me, I only did it because I'm tired."

"I hate jet lag," Graham sympathized. "Sometimes it takes me a week to get over it."

"By that time I'll be ready to go home," she teased. "A good night's sleep will restore my energy."

"Uh, Heather, I'd like to see you again. Is that possible?" he asked shyly.

Her heart beat faster. "Yes, I think so," she smiled. "We do get free time."

"That's nice," he said. "Perhaps I could be your escort. It's more fun to see Jerusalem with a friend. It would be safer in some places, too."

Heather laughed as she remembered Bethlehem's aggressive street vendors. "Our schedule is being revised because of the snowstorm. But I would love to have you show me around Jerusalem."

"Do you know where you'll be tomorrow?" asked Graham.

"Maybe Tiberias because the weather is mild there."

"Tiberias is a fantastic place. Where will you stay?"

"The Caesar Hotel," Heather replied.

"Then I'll call you tomorrow evening," he told Heather. "If you aren't there, I'll call the kibbutz." He smiled broadly.

"Terrific! My room number here is 410. If I'm not in, my roommate, Michelle, can take a message." She paused a bit awkwardly, knowing Graham's father was a short distance away. "Thanks for tonight. I loved the coffee shop, and your dad's real nice."

"I think so too," Graham affirmed. "But he does talk a lot."

Heather gave a laugh. "You should hear *my* father!"

"I'd like that," he said sincerely. "Your brother seems nice."

The teenager wagged her head back and forth to indicate Brian was a mixed blessing. "We get along well most of the time, but we're really different."

"How's that?"

"He's level-headed, and I'm, well, impulsive." They paused for a few seconds, then Heather decided to ask him about the coin's effect on Mr. Ogden. "I hope you don't mind my mentioning this," she began, "but your father looked upset about that French coin. Do you know why?"

Graham wrinkled his brow. "I noticed that, too. I think it's because, as he said, any little thing can break the fragile peace we live with here . . . and because he's close friends with a French diplomat."

She nodded. "Well, thanks again for a fun time."

"You're very welcome." Graham's intense brown eyes held hers for a moment. "I look forward to seeing you again."

Heather floated on a wave of joy through the lobby, where some Kirby students were hanging out. "Here comes Miss America!" one teased.

Heather laughed. "That's exactly how I feel!"

"Have a good time?" Brian came up behind her as he popped open a can of juice.

"Yeah. Real good."

"He's cute," a female Kirby student bubbled. "What's he doing here?"

"His dad's a British diplomat," Heather explained.

A chorus of "oohs" went up from the group. The teenager grinned and went to her room. Before falling asleep, Heather kept thinking, *What a trip! A mystery and romance! I wish Jenn were here! She's going to be so-o-o jealous.* Jenn McLaughlin was Heather's best friend and across-the-street neighbor back home. They were like sisters.

The next morning Dr. Samra lectured on the Roman period and fall of Jerusalem. Heather had rushed to the eight o'clock class only to discover they were "on Israel time." The people at the kibbutz often teased the Americans for being exactly on time for everything. When they said eight o'clock, they meant whenever everyone got there.

After the lecture, the group headed for Tiberias and several famous sites along the way. Their first stop was the Dead Sea caves, where biblical scrolls were discovered after World War II. Heather, Brian, and Joe took a quick hike up into one cave. Then the bus took them down to the sea, where they waded out into heavy salt water up to their knees. Because the elevation was much lower than Jerusalem, the weather here was warm.

Their next destination was Jericho, site of the world's oldest city. From there, the bus whisked them northward to the Roman ruins at Beit Shean and to the Jordan River. They reached their hotel in Tiberias in the late afternoon. Heather loved the remarkable view of the Sea of Galilee from her balcony. She took a swim in the hotel pool before dinner.

In the dining room, Heather learned something about local customs. They were having roast beef, and when she asked for a glass of milk, the waiter's eyes blazed. He walked away muttering something in Hebrew.

"What was that all about?" she asked Dr. Samra, who smiled broadly and explained.

"This hotel is kosher," he said. "You can't have meat and a dairy product on the same table."

Heather frowned. "How was I supposed to know!"

The phone in her room was ringing when she returned after dinner. It was Graham!

"This Saturday the Israeli government is sponsoring a Diplomats' Ball at the King David Hotel," he began. "It's for foreign diplomats and their families, and my father said I could invite you!"

Heather was thrilled. "I'd love to, Graham! But I'll ask my parents before accepting since this will involve buying a special ball dress."

She immediately called her father at work since his day was just beginning. He gave his eager approval, and they talked for a while. "What a great time I'm having!" she told him enthusiastically.

The next day her group took a boat from Tiberias across the Sea of Galilee to the ruins at Capernaum. And after lunch at a nearby kibbutz, the students and professors traveled to Nazareth. The bus crept slowly up the hilly road to the sprawling city toward the Church of Mary's Well. "In ancient times, this was the town's only spring," Dr. Samra explained as the students left the bus.

A group of elderly men wearing *keffiyehs* (traditional Arab headdresses) stood in the church courtyard talking quietly. One of them told Dr. Samra that there was a funeral going on and that the students would have to wait awhile to see the church. Fifteen minutes later a procession of men came somberly out of the church bearing a plain, wooden coffin on their shoulders. A few minutes later the Americans were given permission to go inside.

The church was small but more ornate than any Heather had ever seen before. The richly colored tile mosaics that adorned the walls and floors reminded her of a kaleidoscope. Dr. Coffey talked about the artwork, and Dr. Samra spoke on the church's history. Then they invited the students to explore.

Heather walked with Dr. Samra to the well at the back of the sanctuary. "It's odd to see a spring inside a church," she said. But something more than the water caught Heather's eye. Near the well was a place called the Annunciation Chamber. According to tradition, it was there the angel Gabriel announced to Mary that she would bear Jesus. Heather noticed that parts of the corresponding floor mosaic had been gashed, and a large piece was missing. She knelt down and ran an index finger across the surface. There were still loose fragments in the damaged area, indicating a very recent defacing!

5

Bound and Gagged

W hat are you doing?" the church's priest asked irately.

Heather did look unusual down on her hands and knees. But Dr. Samra intervened, explaining the odd situation to the priest. As he spoke, Heather's eyes scanned the area for signs of the vandal. *Whoever did this to the floor might still be here,* she considered. Just then she spotted a moving shadow in a wall recess. She was about to get up and investigate when the priest cried out in distress.

"Oh, this is terrible!" He put a hand over his heart as if he would die right then and there. "The mosaic is ruined!" He went down on his knees next to Heather.

She stood up as the other Kirby students began to gather around out of curiosity. Dr. Samra briefly explained the situation and asked Brian to get a police officer. He and Joe hurried outside. They quickly returned with one of the ever-present soldiers. The young man listened patiently, his hands resting on the automatic weapon slung around his neck. He hurried off to search the building, only to return several minutes later to say he had found no one suspicious-looking. A few men from the community had also wandered in to catch the news. There was getting to be quite a crowd in the little church.

That's strange, Heather thought. *All these men have dark-complexions, except the one at the back. Too bad I can't see him better.* She pushed her way through the people. But when she reached the courtyard, the man was gone. She looked up and down the narrow streets for several minutes, but to no avail. "Rats!" she mumbled.

"Hey, Heather!" Joe called when she returned to the church. Standing with him was her brother. "We're heading over to a store where the bus driver can get us a discount. Come on!"

She saw other Kirby students chattering outside about what had happened. Heather felt disappointed. While she wanted to go back and search for other clues, she needed to stay with the group.

"Okay, Joe," she told him. "I wonder what that was all about?" She shoved her hands into the pockets of her jeans.

Brian warned her not to get involved. "Forget about it, will you? Stop trying to attract trouble."

"I can't seem to help it." His sister sighed. "We've been in two churches where bizarre things have happened. And both locations are related to the birth of Jesus."

Heather began twisting some hair around a finger, a sure sign that her wheels were spinning.

"Drop it, Heather!" Brian admonished. "This isn't the U.S. It's no place to play detective."

The petite teenager regarded him crossly. "That hurt my feelings! I've done much better than play."

"Okay, okay. I just don't want you getting hurt."

Heather had to laugh. "I won't get hurt." Then she grabbed his arm. "Let's forget all about this nonsense and hunt some bargains at this store Joe's raving about."

His sister's sudden lightheartedness seemed to ease Brian's fears, and he relaxed. But Heather knew in her heart she could never drop a mystery like this.

At the large shop, the Reeds looked for an olive-wood camel to replace the one that had fallen out of the nativity set they bought in Bethlehem. They quickly selected one. While Brian struck a bargain with the shopkeeper, Heather quietly went off to find a restroom. Then Joe came up to the shopkeeper with a necklace he wanted to purchase for his mother.

"That's nice," Brian commented. "Uh, Joe, I don't see Heather and we don't have much time. Would you mind finding her? I want to buy some pita bread from the street vendor before we leave."

"No problem," Joe offered.

"She's probably in the ladies' room," Brian whispered.

"You owe me!" Joe exclaimed and headed off toward the restrooms where he waited several minutes. But Heather didn't come out. What he didn't know was that his friend's sister had met with trouble.

When she had come out of the restroom minutes before, a strong arm reached out and grabbed her from behind. Heather tried to scream for help, but the man's hand quickly clamped her mouth shut. His menacing voice hissed, "Mind your business or you will be the next target!"

His accent sounded French! Heather desperately tried to see his face! But she saw only the edge of his keffiyeh, his hands, and his signet ring with the letter "F."

After pushing her into a nearby utility closet, her assailant gagged her with one keffiyeh and secured her wrists behind her with another. Then he roughly shoved her to the floor and closed the door. He propped a chair under the knob so she couldn't get out.

Heather immediately began chewing on the gag and moving her neck back and forth to loosen it. Five minutes later it fell limply onto her shoulders, and she called out for help. Joe had already left, and with all the customers milling around, it was several more minutes before the shopkeeper heard her cries and set her free.

She thanked him quickly and stuffed the keffiyehs into her pack. The old man raised his hands in a questioning gesture and asked, "What happened?"

"A man gagged me and locked me in the closet," she related. "Did you see him?"

The horrified shopkeeper shook his head.

"He wore a keffiyeh." She produced the one he had used to bind her, but it was no use. Nearly all the men in Nazareth wore them. She hurried off before he could ask more questions.

Heather heard the bus's revving engine and spotted Brian waving impatiently for her to hurry. Then he lectured her about holding things up.

I'd better not let Brian find out what happened, she thought. *He'd be furious!* She sank back into the seat to reflect on the unusual occurrences.

I'll bet that's the same guy from Bethlehem, she pondered. *He seemed to know me. I wonder what in the world he is trying to do?*

"A penny for your thoughts?" Joe asked, tugging Heather's sleeve.

"Nah," she smiled. "These are worth at least a dollar."

He looked at her in surprise but didn't pester her for information. He could tell she didn't want to talk about it, whatever it was. Actually, there was someone Heather would have liked to speak with, and that was Dr. Samra. But several other students had him cornered and were asking about the incident in the church. When she didn't learn anything new from their conversation, Heather closed her eyes for a short nap. But she couldn't sleep. As she reflected on the mysterious man she'd encountered and the ruined church mosaic, Heather thought about the fellow's signet ring. She was certain it was the intital "F." *But did it represent a first or last name?* She pulled the keffiyehs out of her pack and examined them for clues. There were none.

The rest of the day passed uneventfully. After a pleasant

swim and dinner at their hotel, she and a few other Kirby students walked along the shore. Although Heather loved the area, she felt anxious to get back to Jerusalem. Mystery wasn't the only thing on her mind!

In the morning the group headed down the Mediterranean coast on their return trip to Jerusalem. Dr. Samra lectured on the bus, and they made several stops, including the Valley of Jezreel, also known as Megiddo. As the bus approached, the history professor spoke about the area.

"Many battles have been fought here," he announced over the microphone. "They go way back to the time of the Egyptian pharaohs. Then, in the eighteenth century, Napoleon fought here. And in the twentieth century, British General Allenby fought here in the First World War."

Heather stared at the lush green of the valley. It seemed odd to think of wars in such a peaceful-looking place!

"The Bible says history's final battle will occur here," the professor continued. "It's commonly called *Armageddon*, which means 'the hill of Megiddo.' We'll go to the visitors' center on the tell overlooking the valley. A *tell*, by the way, is a manmade hill. We'll examine the scale model of King Solomon's fortress as it was centuries ago. Then we can explore the tell and its fabulous water tunnel."

At the visitors' center Heather quickly became bored with Dr. Samra's rambling talk about King Solomon. But her curiosity was aroused when a group of female tourists entered the room to listen. Oddly, one woman in her twenties wore her sunglasses inside. She also kept glancing in Heather's direction. This continued until the woman walked off by herself.

Michelle tapped Heather's shoulder and made a yawning motion. "Let's get out of here!" she whispered.

Her roommate welcomed the opportunity, hoping to follow the woman in the sunglasses. As it turned out, Michelle was only interested in getting a drink of water and using the restroom. During their absence, however, the two girls missed an announcement by the Megiddo center's curator, Yael Gold, who politely interrupted Dr. Samra.

The middle-aged woman wore a khaki-colored uniform with her badge over one pocket. Her dark hair was tied back in a bushy ponytail. "I am sorry, but we cannot permit you to enter the water tunnel today," she said in her Israeli accent. "Because of the snow we have had recently, the water level is too high. But there are plenty of other attractions. I hope you will enjoy your visit." Then she left, and Dr. Samra ended his lecture.

By the time Heather and Michelle wandered back, the others had gone ahead to explore the tell. They hurried outside and climbed the steep steps to the hill, eager to see the valley from that magnificent height. The others had already been there and were on the other side.

"I need to take pictures," Heather said. "My dad gets as excited as Dr. Samra about this place."

"It's pretty cool," the college girl agreed.

Then they watched as two air-force jets blasted loudly overhead. "If that wasn't eerie!" Heather exclaimed. "After all this talk of war and last battles, it gives me the shivers!"

"Me, too!" Michelle yelled above the noise.

The young women didn't speak for several minutes as they gazed at the panoramic scene. Michelle broke the silence.

"Heather, what's that down there?" She pointed to stone stairs nearby.

"That's where the water tunnel is. Let's take a look!"

"Love to!" Michelle agreed.

They carefully descended the steep, rock-hewn steps, stumbling a few times before they reached the tunnel's entrance, which was a well with more steps. It went down about fifteen feet.

"I guess it's okay to go in," Heather remarked. She pointed to a sign that read, "Tunnel Open."

They walked down into the well, careful of their footing in its murky light. Bare bulbs hung overheard from a wire that stretched the length of the tunnel.

"I hope it isn't too far to the end," Michelle hesitated.

"I don't think it is," Heather reassured her.

A few minutes later the college student cried out, "Hey! My feet are getting wet!"

"Mine are too!" Heather responded, looking down at her own feet. To her horror, rapidly rising water had just topped the wooden walkway!

6

Narrow Escape

T his is so gross!" exclaimed Michelle. She watched as the water lapped first playfully, then aggressively at her low-cut boots. She lifted her long, denim skirt above her knees so it didn't get wet.

Heather chewed her lower lip as she considered the fastest way out. "Let's go all the way to the end," she suggested. "I don't think it's far."

"We'd better hurry. I've never seen water rise this quickly," Michelle replied. She took off across the walkway, which was now completely submerged.

Heather rushed after her. Within a few minutes the water was at her knees!

Suddenly Michelle screamed at the top of her lungs. "Heather! There's no way out!" she hollered.

The startled younger girl quickly gathered her wits and raced ahead.

"I'm coming!" she shouted. When Heather reached her terrified roommate, Michelle pointed toward the end. A shiver ran down Heather's back—the tunnel ended at a stone wall! The raging water mocked their escape effort. "We're trapped!" Michelle panicked. "I'm so scared I could faint!"

"Do that later!" Heather commanded. "I'm scared, too, but we have to think clearly enough to get out of here." She looked for another means of escape, but the rock walls of the tunnel offered none. They would have to swim back.

"I don't swim well," Michelle sobbed.

But there was no other way. In just a few moments the water would literally sweep them off their feet.

"You can use this as a flotation device." Heather handed her backpack to Michelle.

"What about you?"

"I'll swim better without it," she said. "Stay as close to me as you can."

"Heather, I'm getting claustrophobic," Michelle moaned.

"Try to focus on getting out—and pray," Heather advised. "We're going to make it!" She looked into her friend's frightened eyes convincingly, and Michelle began to calm down.

They made slow progress through the treacherous water. Heather tried not to think of her fears of mice and rats. Rodents might also be fleeing the water's wrath. Instead she set her eyes on the light at the beginning of the shaft.

But the situation quickly worsened when the simple string of lights suddenly blinked out. Michelle shrieked

and grabbed Heather's shoulder. Even the brave teenager felt a wave of dread wash over her in that awful
moment. Then she shouted above the water's roar,
"Hold on to me, Michelle!" Although Heather knew she
couldn't go far with the extra weight, it was the only
thing to do. Otherwise Michelle might drown.

Lord, please help! she prayed. A sense of peace gave
Heather fresh hope. Her arms were strengthened, and
her legs kicked powerfully against the water.

But moments later two things happened at once. First
the girls felt their heads strike the top of the tunnel. They
would be completely submerged in moments, and the
entrance was still twenty feet away! But then someone
seized their arms. Now Heather screamed, releasing all
the tension she felt.

"It's okay," a familiar voice called. "It's Tony. Listen to
me."

"Tony!" they cried out. "Thank God!"

"When I finish talking, we're all going to breathe
deeply and go under the water," he instructed. "Hold
onto me, and I'll pull you through. A bunch of people
are at the entrance ready to pull us up. It'll take about
fifteen seconds—then you'll be free. Ready?"

"Yes," they chimed.

"Then—go!"

Heather tucked her head into the turbulent water and
swam furiously. Seconds later Tony let go. The anxiety
she felt lasted only a moment. Then someone pulled her
out of the well. When she rubbed her eyes to get the

water out, Heather saw Joe and several others.

"Joe!" she yelled.

He smiled, then bent down to help Tony and Michelle get out. The rest of the group hurried over to them, accompanied by Doctors Samra and Coffey. When Heather saw Brian run over, she expected the worst. But he surprised her.

"What happened, Heather?" he asked anxiously. But her breathing was so labored she couldn't speak. "Take it easy," he soothed, stroking the long, wet hair out of her eyes.

Finally she blurted out, "I seem destined to spend this trip in wet shoes." She smiled weakly as Brian put his jacket around her shaking shoulders.

"You guys must be really cold," he commented.

The professors were relieved about the rescue but wanted to know why they had gone into the tunnel in the first place.

"We wanted to see it," Heather said innocently.

"But you heard the curator," Dr. Coffey scolded.

Heather and Michelle just looked at each other.

"No, we didn't," the latter remarked.

"She warned us not to go into the tunnel because of the heavy snow they've had," Professor Samra repeated.

"We didn't hear her," Heather admitted. She remembered leaving his boring talk in the visitors' center. Then she added spiritedly, "But the sign said the tunnel was open."

"That's right," Michelle defended.

But the sign now read, "Do not enter!"

The curator joined them, accompanied by two Kirby students who had gone for her. Yael Gold spent the next few minutes talking loudly and animatedly in Hebrew with Dr. Samra. When they finished, Dr. Samra told them, "The curator says she personally put up the warning sign early this morning after inspecting the tunnel."

Heather started to protest but suddenly remembered the mysterious woman who kept staring at her in the visitors' center. She described the stranger to the curator and asked if she'd seen her.

"No, I did not," Yael answered tensely. "I cannot notice everyone who comes here." She seemed relieved when no one challenged her. Then she added, "There was another group here, though. Smaller than yours."

"What kind?" Heather asked, interested.

"A women's club from Jerusalem, I believe," the woman explained. "They were from the French Consulate."

France again! Heather thought. *I'll bet someone in that group knows the guy who threatened me in Nazareth!*

Yael looked at the wet girls with concern. "Please come to my office. You may use my facilities to change your clothes," she offered.

"Brian, will you and Tony please ask the bus driver to open the luggage compartment?" Dr. Samra requested. "Then take the girls' suitcases to the curator's office."

"Sure thing," the young men agreed.

The others milled around, discussing the latest adventure while Heather and Michelle followed Yael Gold to her office.

They hadn't gone very far when Heather noticed something on the grounds that seemed out of place. "Excuse me, Ms. Gold. Look at that hole!"

Yael looked in the direction Heather was pointing and gasped in distress. They walked over and saw a large, freshly-dug hole beside a hollowed-out rock.

"What is going to happen next?" Yael asked, rubbing the back of her hand across her forehead.

"Uh, what is that?" Michelle questioned, shivering.

"It's a manger. Someone is trying to turn this place upside down today!"

"I always pictured mangers as wooden with straw in them," Michelle commented.

Yael answered patiently, "The product of an artist's imagination."

At her office she summoned the maintenance man to find the French tourists. Yael wanted to question them about the incidents. But they had already gone.

Heather felt almost certain now that the woman she'd seen earlier was responsible for both the hole and the near-drowning.

Brian met them at the curator's office a few moments later, and the girls put on clean clothes. Tony had gone to the men's restroom to change. The three students put their wet clothes in plastic bags Yael got for them in the gift shop. As they prepared to leave, she took Heather aside.

"Tell me please, what did this mysterious woman you saw look like?"

"She was in her twenties, had longish auburn hair, and was thin. A bit hard-looking. She also wore her sunglasses inside."

"I don't remember seeing her," Yael said thoughtfully. Then she added, "I pledge to you, I turned that sign to its do-not-enter position."

"I believe you," Heather reassured her.

Then they thanked her and said good-bye. The bus, running behind schedule, hastened to Caesarea. Heather spent the time thinking about the latest drama, hoping Brian wouldn't ask questions. She felt relieved when he did not.

I wonder whether that guy from Nazareth was there, too, Heather considered. *I'm sure he and the woman in the sunglasses are working together. Hmm . . . Mangers remind me of Christmas and nativity scenes.* She stared out the window for a few minutes. *It was the real manger scene in Bethlehem that was disturbed, then the mosaic near the place where Mary discovered she'd have a baby.*

But Heather was clueless about why these things had happened. She drifted off to sleep and awakened in Caesarea, where they got off the bus and looked at an ancient Roman aqueduct along the Mediterranean shore. Then they went to lunch. And even though they had to hurry, Heather still enjoyed the seasoned chicken and rice, fresh fruit salad, and tea.

They had one more stop before returning to Jerusalem. But it presented another problem. At the admissions gate to an old Roman theater, a female soldier gave the

American professors bad news. Heather stood close behind them to find out what was going on.

"I am sorry, but if you want to go in, you must wait at least thirty minutes," the woman insisted.

"What's wrong?" Dr. Samra wanted an explanation.

"As I told you, it was just a small incident," she contended.

"There are too many authorities around for it to be small, young lady," the professor commented. "Our group paid to see this, and we can't wait."

The woman gestured to another soldier. When he came over, they conversed briefly in Hebrew. Then he turned to the professors. "An old stone was overturned a short time ago."

Heather felt excited. *I wonder if there's a connection with this and Megiddo?* she wondered. She peaked out from behind the professors and asked boldly, "What kind of stone was it?"

The female soldier regarded her intensely, then addressed her partner. Finally she told the Americans, "It was the stone of Pontius Pilate."

7

Search for Vandals

As the bus journeyed back to Jerusalem, many students took naps. Heather felt stiff from the water tunnel ordeal. The rest of the Kirby group was mildly curious about the bizarre happenings they'd witnessed, but Heather was directly involved. She wanted to solve what she believed were related mysteries.

"Heather," Dr. Samra called quietly so he didn't awaken any sleepers. She turned from the window and her reflections. The plump professor sat down next to her. "Feeling better?"

"Other than a little stiffness, I'm fine," she said.

"I'm still pretty worked up about that tunnel bit," he said. "It's as if someone deliberately tried to harm you and Michelle. And then there were those unusual incidents in Nazareth and Caesarea."

Heather wanted to discuss these matters with him. And she could trust him not to tell Brian. She knew her brother would only worry and try to put a stop to her investigation.

"I'm bothered by something else," Dr. Samra continued.

"What's that?"

"That Pontius Pilate stone—it's worthless," Dr. Samra stated.

Heather perked right up. "Worthless?"

"It's only a copy of the original, which is in a British museum," he said.

"You're beginning to sound like me," Heather teased.

Dr. Samra smiled. He understood her love of mysteries. Then he leaned closer. "I know what you're up to, my girl," he said sternly. Then he added smiling, "And you can trust me not to let Brian in on it."

"That's a relief," Heather responded.

"So, why did someone try to drown you and Michelle?" he asked. "Has your reputation as an amateur detective followed you here?"

"I doubt it," she smiled. "But I could've angered that thief I tried to catch in Bethlehem, especially if he gashed the mosaic in Nazareth, too." Then Heather told the professor about the warning she received in Nazareth.

"That explains the tunnel then," he frowned. "Heather, I must insist that you stay with the group from now on." He smirked playfully. "I saw you and Michelle leave when I rambled on at the visitors' center."

"Sorry," she apologized.

"I take no offense. In fact, I bore myself at times." He nudged her affectionately, and she laughed softly.

"Maybe you can help me figure something out," Heather invited.

"I'll certainly try." He crossed his arms over his ample chest.

"At Bethlehem and then with the manger at Megiddo, there are reminders of Jesus' birth," she mused quietly. "And Pilate sentenced Jesus to death. I think these people are looking for something valuable related to the birth—and maybe the death—of Jesus. But what?"

"I don't know," he admitted after a few moments. "It has me perplexed."

The bus arrived in Jerusalem behind schedule. Since the dining room would only remain open fifteen minutes longer, everyone rushed to dinner. Although Heather would have liked to call Graham, she felt tired and went to bed early.

The following morning she showered and went to breakfast before the others. She wanted to get a copy of the *Jerusalem Post* to see if there was a story about the acts of vandalism she had witnessed. To her delight, Heather discovered an article on the third page describing the Pilate stone incident. At the end it read, "Authorities are investigating similar events in other historic places over the last few days. According to one report, two American students nearly drowned in the water tunnel on the Megiddo tell after a warning sign was mysteriously turned to the safe-passage side. The two students escaped unharmed."

Heather folded the paper and laid it on the seat next to her. *I must talk to Graham!* she thought.

But she had to wait until the afternoon because her group had an appointment to hear a guest lecture at the Hebrew University at nine o'clock. Then they would have lunch at the school's cafeteria.

When they returned to the kibbutz at one-thirty that afternoon, the woman at the front desk handed Heather a message. Graham had called to say he'd come by at seven-thirty. She used the house phone to call the Ogdens' and left a message with their housekeeper for Graham to bring his bathing suit. Heather wanted to swim that night and also thought it would afford them privacy from her brother.

As for the rest of the afternoon, she had some shopping to do. The woman at the front desk suggested the fashionable Ben Yehuda district and told Heather and Michelle how to get there. The Americans thanked her and went right out to catch a city bus.

At the street "mall," they enjoyed browsing through big and small shops and listening to Russian emigrant musicians perform outside. They were amazed by the security in one department store. When the two American girls entered, a uniformed guard took their packs and told them to walk through a metal detector. "Bomba," he explained. Although the possibility of having a bomb go off there caused her some anxiety, Heather found a beautiful formal ball dress and accessories at that store.

It was a simple but elegant black gown covered with tiny sequins. The petite teenager looked very attractive in the dress's classic lines.

The clerk also assisted Heather in purchasing accessories to complete the outfit—jewelry, shoes, and a handbag. And in addition, the saleswoman asked if Heather would like to rent a special evening wrap.

"That would be wonderful!" the sixteen-year-old exclaimed. "I'd hate to put my raincoat over this elegant ensemble."

"I will have everything sent to your hotel Friday morning," the clerk promised after Heather paid for the purchases.

That evening Mr. Ogden drove his son to the kibbutz on the way to a meeting. Graham and Heather went to the pool and talked for a while before swimming. She told him about the outfit she bought and how excited she was about the upcoming ball. Then Graham narrowed his eyes, and his voice dropped to a confidential tone.

"I was worried when I read about the near-drowning in this morning's paper," he said. "I had this fear you were involved. That was silly, wasn't it?"

"No, that was us," Heather stated bluntly.

Graham's soft brown eyes widened in disbelief. "It was?"

For a fleeting moment Heather was worried that Mr. Ogden might be using his son to gain information from her. *He must know what goes on at the various embassies,* she considered. *What if he is involved in these weird happenings?*

But Nigel Ogden hadn't struck Heather as a dishonest man. She decided to trust Graham and give his father the benefit of the doubt. So she told the British teenager all about the odd occurrences. Heather eagerly waited for him to comment.

After some time he said, "I, too, believe there's a search on for something of great value. And I agree it's probably connected with the life of Jesus."

"Any ideas?" Heather asked, hugging her knees to her chest.

"A few, but they're just off the top of my head."

"Like what?" she pursued.

"Oh, it could be on the order of 'the true cross,' which some people try selling to unsuspecting tourists. Or the actual manger Mary laid him in after his birth."

Heather wasn't so sure. "Maybe," she said cautiously. She didn't want to hurt her friend's feelings.

Graham fell into silent reflection. Minutes later he shook his head and chuckled. "I'm reading a book for school about King Arthur. Although it sounds ridiculous, I'll say it anyway."

"What is it?" Heather encouraged. "It helps to brainstorm."

Graham took a deep breath. "Wouldn't it be something if the vandals were looking for the Holy Grail!"

8

The Eerie Echo

The Grail," Heather repeated thoughtfully. "I vaguely remember a movie about King Arthur and the Grail. How much do you know about it?"

Actually, Graham knew a lot. "I've always been interested in the legends of the Grail," he told his new friend. "Maybe it's part of growing up in England."

"You mean the Knights of the Round Table and all that?" Heather inquired.

"Exactly. I love the stories." He paused. "My mother used to read them to me." Heather put a comforting hand on his arm, and Graham smiled. Then he proceeded. "I'm sure you know the Grail was the cup used by Jesus at the Last Supper."

"Yes," Heather said. "I just don't know what happened to it."

"That's what people have been wondering for centuries. There are lots of myths, most of them too fantastic to take seriously. But there are common themes in the most important ones. For example, most of them say the

Cup was also used to catch the blood of Jesus at his crucifixion."

Heather wrinkled her nose. "How totally gross!"

"It is repulsive," he admitted. "The Grail was entrusted to Joseph of Arimathea, the man who owned the tomb where Jesus was buried. Some say he laid the cup in the grave, too, and that's what gave Jesus power to rise from the dead."

"I never heard that one before," Heather remarked.

"The stories get even more peculiar," Graham commented. "One says Joseph was imprisoned for forty years, but the Grail kept him in a state of rapture. After his release, Joseph gave it to a friend. Both went to Britain as missionaries, and that's where the story becomes muddled. When King Arthur ruled in the sixth century, his Knights of the Round Table went on two quests to find the Grail. Though none of them could possess it, Percival saw it."

"Are you saying someone first wrote about the Grail in King Arthur's time?" The stories Graham was telling fascinated Heather.

"Actually nothing was written about the Grail for a thousand years after Christ's death."

"A thousand years!" she exclaimed.

"That's right. Most of the stories involved King Arthur. But they were so exaggerated that not until recently have scholars believed Arthur even lived."

"And no one knows what happened to the Grail?"

"That's right," Graham stated. "But people have gone to incredible lengths to find it. They believed it would cure any sickness or make a person live forever."

"Graham," Heather said, "maybe your idea isn't crazy."

"You mean that the vandals are looking for the Grail?"

"Yes. If you think about it, all the places are connected to either Christ's death or birth," she explained.

"True, but Heather, there are hundreds of places like that in Israel," Graham remarked.

"Well, someone could be scheming to turn them upside down looking for the Grail."

He smiled broadly. "You sound like a detective."

"The truth is, I have done some amateur work," she said modestly.

"I'll bet you'd like to solve this mystery!" Graham exclaimed.

"You bet! In fact, I have a few more clues."

Heather told him about the man with the French accent who tied her up and warned her not to interfere. Then she mentioned the woman who probably switched the sign at Megiddo.

"She was with a group from the French Embassy," Heather added. "There's definitely a French connection here. Remember the coin I found?"

"I do. I might have mentioned my father is best friends with a French diplomat."

"You did," Heather said. "And your dad mentioned he'd check things out. Did he discover anything?"

"I guess not. That is, he didn't say anything to me. But I'm sure you could find out for yourself," he suggested.

"What?"

"He could get us an appointment!"

"That would be super!" she exclaimed. "By the way, what is his name?" She was thinking of the "F" on her attacker's ring in Nazareth.

"Francois Gilbert," Graham answered. "Are you thinking of the initial 'F'?" he inquired.

Heather became grim. "Yes. Although signet rings usually refer to the last name."

"I can assure you, Mr. Gilbert is a splendid person," Graham added. "Maybe he can help you."

Maybe, Heather thought. Experience had taught her not to rule out any suspect until evidence proved otherwise.

When Mr. Ogden picked his son up, Graham asked him to arrange a meeting with Francois Gilbert. The diplomat slapped a palm to his forehead. "I completely forgot about that! I'm awfully sorry," he apologized. "I'll call Francois, but I can't promise anything. He's had a bad time of it. His grandfather died in Paris a few weeks ago. Heather, are there times when you're available?" he asked. She told him her schedule for the rest of the trip.

"He most likely won't have answers for you," the Englishman said skeptically "but I think you'll enjoy meeting him. He's a delightful person, and he comes from an old, celebrated French family."

"Thank you," Heather responded, feeling satisfied that Mr. Ogden was innocent. Otherwise he wouldn't be so eager to help. *That's a relief!* she thought. *I really like him.*

The next morning both Dr. Samra and Dr. Coffey spoke on the Crusades of the Middle Ages. Then the Kirby College group took their chartered bus to places in Jerusalem associated with the Crusader period.

Their first stop was the majestic Al Aqsa mosque on the Temple Mount, across from the even more beautiful Dome of the Rock.

"During the Crusades, an elite society of French warrior-monks called the Knights Templar used the mosque as their headquarters," Dr. Samra said. Heather was especially interested in the mosque's link to French knights.

Just then loud voices came from inside. Everyone turned to listen, and Dr. Samra called them back to attention. When he finished, Heather quietly found a security guard and asked the cause of the shouting.

He was very excited and told her in broken English, "Last night we see a man near here going back and forth, back and forth."

"What was he doing?" she asked.

The man threw his hands up. "Who knows! But we be very careful. Too much else happening."

"What did he look like?" she pursued, wondering if this were related to the other incidents.

"Ah, I no here then. Others tell me he is European."

"Did you catch him?"

But just then Dr. Samra noticed what she was doing. "Heather! Hurry up!" he called out.

Brian glared at her impatiently. But the spirited teenager wouldn't give up until she got an answer. "Did you catch him?" she repeated.

"No. He get away."

Heather thanked him and rushed back to her gang. *I wish I knew more about what happened with that man,* she thought.

Their next stop was the Church of St. Anne next to the Pool of Bethesda in the Old City. The neighborhood gave Heather the creeps. Tough-looking vendors approached them. They yelled angrily when the Americans refused to buy their items.

As they neared the nine-hundred-year-old church, Brian pointed to a beggar holding out a chipped glass. "Will you look at that?" The man's left leg looked as though insects had eaten parts of it. Heather paled and turned away. Several other Kirby students blanched and hurried on.

Joe patted her shoulder and whispered, "It's fake, Heather. A makeup job."

Her hazel eyes opened wide. "A makeup job!"

Brian shrugged. "I guess it's a living."

Then a nervous-looking priest in a white robe rushed to meet the Americans. "Welcome to St. Anne's," he said, but his manner was strained. He told the college professors, "We cannot permit tours of the church today, but please enjoy the grounds."

"But why . . . ?" Dr. Coffey's question went unanswered as the priest hastily slipped away. "I wanted so much for you to see the Crusader architecture," she complained. "The French did such a great job here."

The French again! Heather thought. Suddenly she had to get inside. She was certain something fishy was going on in there. While the others roamed the fascinating porches and columns of the Pool of Bethesda, Heather again snuck away.

At the church's entrance she quickly looked around, making sure no one saw her. Then the impish teenager slipped inside.

It took several seconds for her eyes to adjust in the dim light. Then she saw the outlines of an imposing sanctuary with dozens of pews, very few windows and a remarkably high ceiling.

She carefully advanced down the aisle and had taken just a few steps when she heard something that made her flesh crawl. A ghostlike voice echoed through the dark, old building, then bounced off the vaulted ceiling and around the walls—"Turn back or die!"

9

Suspects in the Consulate

Heather endured a wave of panic, sensing the voice was a hoax. But for all her bravery, she weakened under the echo's incessant ricochet against the aged walls. She fled the church, welcoming the sunlight.

The sixteen-year-old stood quietly and waited for her speeding heart to slow down. But even then, her thoughts raced. *I just know this is linked to the other things that have happened. And that priest doesn't know what to do about the echo. It's clearly meant for anyone going inside, not just me.* But another thought made her reconsider. *The voice spoke in English. Did whoever speak realize it was me? I must find out what's going on!*

Heather squared her shoulders and joined the group in exploring the ancient pool. To her relief, no one had missed her. *Could someone hide in these ruins?* she wondered. However, she concluded that the numerous porches and platforms were both too public and too small to conceal a person. But one cavelike section was so dark inside that Heather, standing with Michelle and Tony, couldn't see beyond the entrance.

"If I could just find my flashlight." Tony rummaged through his backpack. "Here it is!" he exclaimed.

He turned its powerful beam on, revealing slimy walls, thick cobwebs and a spooky-looking pool. Though wide, the cave was not long. It stopped abruptly at an imposing rock wall.

"I wonder how deep it is," Michelle trembled.

Dr. Samra joined them and answered the question. "I don't know about this part, but some of the pools are eighty feet deep."

Heather shuddered, reminded of the Megiddo tunnel. She and Michelle exchanged a knowing look.

In the early afternoon, Graham took a bus to the Kibbutz Yehuda and found Heather in the coffee shop with Joe and Brian. He had news about the French diplomat but waited to share it until the guys left. Heather had told him about her overly-protective brother.

"Your father must have talked to Mr. Gilbert," she said enthusiastically.

"He did, and we have an appointment today at four o'clock!" His pleasant eyes sparkled.

"That's wonderful!" she exclaimed. Then she lowered her voice. "I have news as well." And she told her handsome friend about the strange episode at St. Anne's. "Have you ever been there?"

"I'm not sure," he reflected. "I've visited many historic churches in Jerusalem—they run together after a while."

The girl shook her head. "You'd remember this one. The church, the pool, and the neighborhood are like something out of a black and white movie. On our way out an old woman selling purses approached Brian. He teased her, saying he'd buy one for half what she was asking. But she cursed him!"

"Cursed him?" Graham repeated.

"Uh-huh. Then these guys gave us threatening looks, so we got on the bus in a hurry."

"Definitely not nice," he remarked. Then he checked his watch. "We've got an hour and a half before our meeting. Dad said he'd catch up with us there."

"I'm really glad you're interested in this mystery," she smiled.

"It's great fun!" he said in his terrific British accent. Then Graham added, "I'm pleased you trust my father, too. You know he's concerned about Mr. Gilbert. He's been deeply affected by his grandfather's death, and Dad thinks someone at the consulate might be taking advantage of that to commit these weird crimes."

"Hmm," Heather mused, twisting a lock of hair. "Do you think the authorities suspect anyone at the consulate, or that the Grail may be involved?"

"I believe you're several steps ahead of anyone else," Graham responded. Then he added with a smile, "In more ways than one."

Heather blushed. But then a brainstorm hit, and she suddenly announced, "Let's go to Bethlehem! Maybe the priest can tell us more about the man who tried to steal the star."

The British teenager agreed. "A marvelous idea!"

When they arrived in Bethlehem thirty minutes later, they noticed many soldiers roaming alertly through the tourists and merchants in Manger Square.

"They aren't taking any chances," Heather whispered. Graham nodded.

A male and a female soldier met each person entering the Church of the Nativity and walked them through a metal detecting booth. Then they skillfully frisked them. When they got through, the teenagers went in search of Father Dimitri. Heather gave Graham the best description she could of the priest, but . . .

"This is hard," Graham admitted after ten minutes. "Their robes and dark beards make them look alike."

"I know what you mean," she agreed.

To their surprise, Father Dimitri found them. He spotted Heather as she walked past a souvenir stand.

"The American girl!" he exclaimed.

"Father Dimitri! I came to see you."

"I am so very happy." He shook both of her hands at once. "I must tell you something."

In her enthusiasm Heather nearly forgot Graham. Then she recovered her manners and introduced him to the cleric.

"I want you to follow me," he requested. The young priest led them to a wall mosaic of the Madonna and Child.

Heather gasped and pointed. "Wasn't there a lot of jewelry there?"

"Yes, yes," he said. "Pilgrims often leave their trinkets to honor the Holy Family. After we talked to the authorities about the star, we discovered this theft."

Graham was upset. "What a dishonorable thing to do!"

"Yes, it was," Father Dimitri agreed. "People leave that jewelry as a token of worship."

"Did you find out anything else about that thief?" Heather asked.

"I know nothing more." His dark eyes looked both sad and angry. "The police say they are still searching for him." He frowned. "You are not trying to find this man?"

"I'm just a nosy person," she laughed.

A slight grin lightened Father Dimitri's dusky face. "Thank you for caring enough to return."

Back outside, Heather said, "I keep thinking the Bethlehem thief and the guy at Nazareth are one and the same."

"Whoever he is, he's a greedy, mean-spirited person," Graham stated.

They took the bus back to Jerusalem and arrived at the French Consulate just as Mr. Ogden emerged from the parking garage. They would have to wait till later to tell Graham's father about their side trip to Bethlehem. Inside the ornate foyer, Mr. Ogden led them to the elevator and got off on the eighth floor. A young French secretary with long auburn hair greeted them. She appeared to be in her early twenties and was wearing a stylish skirt and sweater. Although she was attractive, Heather thought she looked hard. *She certainly doesn't seem too friendly.*

"Hello, Mr. Ogden," she greeted.

"Good afternoon, Edith," he replied. "I'd like you to meet my son, Graham, and his American friend, Heather Reed. This is Edith Trottier."

Heather suddenly realized Mr. Gilbert's secretary was the strange woman from Megiddo!

10

Deceptive Diplomat

The teenager pretended she had never seen Edith Trottier before and greeted her politely. *What other secrets will this visit reveal?* she wondered.

"Please follow me," the secretary instructed crisply. She led the visitors into a large office where the strikingly handsome Francois Gilbert received them.

"Nigel! Graham!" He welcomed them gladly with an outstretched hand.

"This is our new American friend, Heather Reed. Heather, Mr. Francois Gilbert."

"Hello," she responded.

Mr. Gilbert took her hand. "I am happy to meet you."

Heather subtly looked down. *He's wearing a signet ring!* She tried to contain her excitement and glanced again. *It says "G,"* she thought. *At least Francois Gilbert isn't the thief,* she concluded.

Then Edith Trottier left the office, but not before giving the girl a harsh look. *I wonder if she knows I've seen her before?* Heather considered.

They all sat on delicate French Provincial chairs, and Heather studied Francois Gilbert. He was around forty years old and of medium height and weight. His gray-blue eyes, well-trimmed mustache, and short brown hair enhanced the piercing effect of his features. Even the suit, shirt, and tie he wore had a sharp quality. His tastefully furnished office suited him well. For all that, however, he looked tired and stressed.

Heather glanced at Mr. Ogden and grinned. Next to his elegant friend, Graham's father looked downright rumpled. His clothes were an afterthought, and his hair hadn't been combed recently. But he was completely unaware of the contrast.

"Thank you for seeing us today," he said.

Mr. Gilbert crossed his legs. "It is always a pleasure." His words were beautifully accented, unlike the man's in Nazareth or the ghostly voice at St. Anne's.

"But this hasn't been an easy time for you," Mr. Ogden sympathized.

A dark look passed across Mr. Gilbert's face, and he said awkwardly, "Yes, well . . . to what do I owe this pleasure?"

"Heather is in Israel with a college group, and she's been having quite an adventure." Mr. Ogden smiled in her direction. "Please tell Francois about it."

On the way back from Bethlehem she and Graham had decided to paint the picture with broad strokes. She began with the story about the Church of the Nativity and the star.

"And you chased the man?" Gilbert asked, amazed. "You are courageous!"

"Thank you," she accepted. Heather had a strange feeling the Frenchman had already heard this story. She proceeded carefully.

"Did you catch him?" he asked, cocking his head in an engaging way.

"No. But he dropped something." She handed him the French coin.

Gilbert tried vainly to conceal his alarm. He held the object as if it were a hot potato.

"The man may have been French," Graham commented.

The diplomat laughed slightly. Heather could tell he didn't mean it, though. "Anyone can carry French money," he shrugged.

"I agree, Mr. Gilbert," Heather said. "But then something else happened."

Although the refined man looked composed, a trace of fear flickered in his eyes. "And what was that?"

"In Nazareth the other day, a man with a French accent threatened to harm me if I didn't mind my business. It had to be either the man from the Church of the Nativity or someone who knew him."

Gilbert looked genuinely startled. Heather continued.

"Then we went to the tell at Megiddo. I didn't hear the curator say to my group not to go into the water tunnel. Well, my roommate and I went in because the sign said it was open." She paused for dramatic effect. "We nearly drowned."

He was genuinely shocked. "That is terrible!" he exclaimed. "I am so glad you got out."

"So am I!" she stated. "While we were at the visitors' center at Megiddo, a group of ladies arrived. They were on a tour sponsored by the French Consulate. One woman kept staring at me. She didn't seem happy to see me either. I believe she turned the sign around deliberately." Heather stopped short of telling him it had been Edith Trottier.

"But why would someone do such a thing?" he cried out.

"She must have been partners with the man who threatened me earlier," Heather replied. "There's more. After our escape, my roommate and I noticed a freshly dug hole beside a stone manger."

Gilbert looked deflated. "No true Frenchman would do such things," he muttered, clenching his right hand into a fist.

"Sounds like you might have some loose cannons around," Nigel Ogden remarked. Noticing his friend's distress, he said, "Well, I don't want to overstay our welcome, Francois. You look tired."

The Frenchman made another weak effort at smiling. "I will look into this matter, Miss Reed," he promised. "Your story upsets me greatly." There was no mistaking his sincerity.

Mr. Ogden heaved his heavy bulk out of the dainty chair, and it creaked rather loudly. He laughed at himself. "We don't have furniture like this in England."

His friend gave a laugh, too, grateful for the comic relief. Heather took advantage of his sudden good humor to ask another question.

"Mr. Gilbert, could you tell me anything about St. Anne's Church near the Pool of Bethesda?"

"What would you like to know?" he asked stiffly, his face suddenly gone pale.

"Anything! I just saw it and was so fascinated. The priest wouldn't let us inside, though. All I really know is that it was built by French crusaders."

The diplomat leaned against the front of his desk for support and tried to politely answer the girl's question. "It is the only church built during the Crusades that survived them," he began. "St. Anne's passed into Moslem hands when the warrior Saladin took over Jerusalem. It remained under various Moslem governments until, let me see, the eighteenth century. One hundred years later the French government accepted St. Anne's from the Ottoman Turks, who ruled the Middle East then. A few years later the White Fathers, an African missionary order, agreed to run it."

"So is St. Anne's still French?" Heather asked.

"That is correct," Gilbert said, hoping she was satisfied.

"Even though the White Fathers administer the church, doesn't it still belong to France and have the same status as an embassy?" asked Mr. Ogden.

"That is so," his friend responded.

"That's very interesting." Heather said. Then Heather took the plunge and told Gilbert what had happened to her at the church. Both he and Nigel Ogden looked unsettled.

"You do find adventures, young lady!" Gilbert commented. "I am grateful you have not been hurt. I promise to check out these things and get in touch with you." He paused then asked, "Where are you staying?"

"At the Kibbutz Yehuda," she answered.

"A very nice hotel. And how long will you stay?"

"Only a few more days," she said.

"Long enough to go to the ball with me," Graham added enthusiastically.

"I'm really looking forward to that," she smiled.

"I will see you then at the ball and tell you what I can," Gilbert decided.

Just then Graham's gaze fell upon a fascinating old book on the man's desk. He picked it up and opened it. But the French diplomat lunged at him. "Put that down!" he commanded.

11

Deadly Quest

Graham nearly dropped the old volume in his surprise over Gilbert's tone of voice. He quickly and carefully put the book back. "We'd better go, Dad," he urged.

But Mr. Ogden wanted an explanation first. "Francois, are you really all right?" He placed a hand on his friend's shoulder. "If you're not, I want to help you. Otherwise, you owe my son an apology."

The Frenchman hung his head. "Graham, you must please forgive my rude outburst. Though I have been disturbed of late, it is no excuse for shrieking at a friend. Forgive me?"

"Yes," the kindhearted teenager said. "You must have been close to your grandfather."

Gilbert looked straight at Graham, then sighed. "One could say that. But I have been left with much responsibility."

"Maybe we shouldn't have troubled you," Nigel Ogden declared. He smiled at Heather and his son. "Time to go."

Heather believed Gilbert's unsteadiness was due to more than his relative's death. But she shook his hand and considerately thanked him for his time.

He bowed slightly. "I am glad that I met you. I hope the rest of your trip is pleasurable. Perhaps you should be more cautious." His eyes held hers for a moment.

Is this a friendly warning? Heather wondered, more suspicious than ever.

"We hope to show her a wonderful time at the ball," Mr. Ogden declared, winking at Heather.

Gilbert paused at the door with his visitors. "Then I will see you tomorrow night."

"Who are you going with?" his friend asked.

"This time I will go alone."

When they left, the American teenager felt Edith Trottier's gaze follow her out of the office. As Heather walked into the cold afternoon air, she couldn't help wishing she could see what was going on back there now!

Nigel Ogden was also reflecting deeply. In the parking garage, he paused over his locked car door. "Nah," he said absently. But when they got inside, he asked, "Do you think Francois knows anything about these odd circumstances? I've never seen him like that."

Graham said, "Maybe, Dad. He was uptight about our questions and really hit the roof over that book."

"I know," Mr. Ogden replied, "but then I remember Francois is an honorable man."

"Did you get a look at the title?" Heather asked Graham.

He leaned forward, against the backs of the driver's and passenger's seats. "Come to think of it, I don't think it had one."

"Whatever it was, he didn't want us to see it," Heather concluded. "Right now, though, I'm more troubled about Edith Trottier. I've been dying to tell you—she's the woman I saw at Megiddo!"

"What a discovery!" Graham shouted. "And she's working for Mr. Gilbert."

"This really is awful," his father murmured as he pulled onto the busy street.

Heather was grim. "Mr. Ogden, what do you know about her?"

"Not much. She has only been working with Francois since last spring."

Heather sat quietly for some minutes thinking about the mystery. *Gilbert doesn't seem like a criminal. But I get the impression he knows something more than he's saying,* she pondered. *As for Edith Trottier, she's number one on my list of suspects. But who's the other French guy? And what are they really after?*

Mr. Ogden didn't say much on the way to the kibbutz. When he pulled up to the entrance, he made an effort at cheerfulness. "Tomorrow should be a fun day, Heather. I'd like you to have at least one happy memory to take back home with you."

"I already have many," she beamed. "Though I'm sure the ball will be my best."

"You enjoy adventure, don't you?" he asked.

"She's solved some mysteries, haven't you, Heather?" Graham commented proudly.

"A couple," she responded.

"A teenage detective!" the English diplomat exclaimed lightly. "Then you really must be enjoying your trip."

"Yes," she agreed. "Especially the new friends I've made. And thank you for making that appointment with Mr. Gilbert."

Suddenly Mr. Ogden's frown returned. "You're quite welcome."

Then Heather added, "Mr. Gilbert doesn't seem like a bad person."

"I assure you, he isn't," Mr. Ogden asserted. "But I can tell he is deeply troubled about something."

Heather agreed. "If you talk to him and think there's anything worth passing along, please let me know," Heather requested.

"I can't imagine what this is all about."

"Actually, Graham has an idea about that," the American teenager said. "I'm sure he'll explain it on your way home."

Graham blushed but seemed to appreciate the compliment. "Can we get together in the morning?" he asked hopefully.

"Sure. That is, if we can search for more clues."

They eagerly made plans. Mr. Ogden would be busy until the late afternoon, so Graham said they could use public transportation to get around the ancient city.

Heather awakened early the next day and went for a refreshing swim before breakfast. She loved the sport and always took advantage of any pool she was near. Then she showered, dressed in jeans and a ribbed sweater, and went to the dining room where she sat with Michelle and Tony. *I'm glad Brian isn't here,* she reflected. *He'd want to know my plans.*

After a healthy meal of freshly-picked fruit, a large blueberry muffin, and hot cereal, Heather felt ready for action. Most of the other students planned to stay at the kibbutz and relax. Saturday was the sabbath day in Israel, and many places they might have visited would be closed.

Graham came for her on the bus just after nine, and they immediately headed into the Old City. He shared a plan with Heather, and she approved.

"Since the suspects may be searching for the Holy Grail," he said, "let's visit some sites connected with the crucifixion."

"To see if they've had any incidents?" Heather asked.

"Exactly. Let's go to the Upper Room first, then trace the route Jesus took from there to his death."

"Good idea!" she praised him.

At the Upper Room Heather learned the chamber was not the original. It was simply a large, empty hall with several highly-placed windows. A man who lived nearby told the couple nothing unusual had happened there recently. Satisfied, they took another bus to the Garden of Gethsemane, where Jesus had been arrested.

They asked the attending priest about any strange incidents.

"Oh, yes!" he exclaimed, and their hearts beat faster. "In Bethlehem a thief tried to steal the star from the holy grotto."

"We already . . . " Heather's voice trailed off as he interrupted her.

"And in Nazareth a mosaic was destroyed. But the worst thing was when the water tunnel at Megiddo filled, and a bus load of tourists nearly drowned!"

The young people thought they would die holding back their laughter. Graham quickly thanked the priest, and they hurried outside. Then they let go and howled!

On the next bus ride, Heather felt as if she and Graham were being followed. At first it was only a hunch. Then wherever the two of them went, Heather kept seeing a young woman of the same build and height as Edith Trottier. However, because she wore large sunglasses and a knit hat wrapped around her head and neck, the woman could have been someone else. *Maybe an accomplice,* she thought. *But I doubt it.*

When Heather alerted her friend, he whispered, "I've noticed her, too."

Next they went to a church commemorating Jesus' trial, then to the Via Dolorosa, where he carried the cross to his death. No disturbances were reported in either place by the nuns or priests. But the mysterious woman continued shadowing them.

However, at the Church of the Holy Sepulchre the priest they talked to was quite troubled. He told them that very early in the morning at the Garden Tomb of Jesus, the watchman saw someone trying to blow-torch his way into the tomb! The guard startled the man but couldn't catch him.

"What did he look like?" Heather asked.

"And why do you want to know?" The priest put his hands on his hips and looked at her skeptically.

She quickly thought of something. "In America we have TV shows that describe criminals so ordinary people can help catch them," she offered. Graham was so tickled by the clever comeback that he coughed into his hand to muffle a laugh.

The priest accepted the explanation and shared what he knew. The guard had said the man wore black and had a knit cap on his head. He was of medium size, about forty, with a brown mustache.

Heather and Graham turned toward each other and blurted, "Mr. Gilbert!"

12

A Fairy-Tale Evening

As the teenagers rode in a cab on their way to the kibbutz, they considered this latest development.

"I find it unbelievable that Mr. Gilbert would do such a thing." Graham shook his handsome head.

Heather glanced nervously out the rear window. "I wonder if we're still being followed?" she asked aloud.

"I haven't noticed her for a while," Graham commented. "You're pretty sure it was Edith Trottier?"

"Though we didn't get a good look at her face, I have a strong hunch it was. Graham," she asked, "how well do you know Mr. Gilbert?"

"Pretty well, I think. He's always been nice to me, and my father thinks highly of him. Why?"

"You told me once that people have gone to great lengths to find the Holy Grail," she reminded him. "If our guess is right about this Grail hunt and he's part of it, that could explain his behavior. I just wish we could've seen what was in that book."

Graham scowled. "Whatever it was, he definitely didn't want us to see it."

"I'm wondering how Francois Gilbert would have information about the Grail."

"I have no idea. But Heather," he looked into her bright hazel eyes, "I don't distrust him."

This surprised her. "Even now?"

He closed his eyes and nodded, his lips pursed. "Yes. He's a good man overall. I doubt he'd hurt anyone. You saw how upset he was when he learned of your ordeals."

Heather didn't respond. *Maybe he wouldn't hurt anyone,* she thought, *but somehow he's involved.*

Later that afternoon Heather began her preparations for the Diplomats' Ball. First she took a relaxing bubble bath, but cut it short when Michelle summoned her to the phone. Mr. and Mrs. Reed and Heather's best friend, Jenn, were calling from home. They took turns speaking for ten minutes.

"Have a wonderful time!" her mother concluded happily. "And make sure Brian takes lots of pictures," her father added.

"Though I'm green with envy," Jenn told her, "I'm thrilled for you and hope you'll have the night of your life." Before hanging up she said, "For once you've chosen romance over mystery!"

Heather was glad they didn't know what was really going on! And since Brian wasn't in the room, he couldn't tell them either.

At seven-thirty Heather was dressed and ready for her big evening. The excited teenager took the elevator to the lobby where she was completely startled by thunderous applause and the sound of cameras clicking and whirring. She had expected Brian, Joe, and Dr. Samra to be there for pictures, but everyone else from Kirby had shown up as well!

Joe walked up to her with a hair brush he pretended was a microphone. "Princess Heather, may we have a few words?"

"This is incredible!" she laughed into the "mike." Then Brian led Graham, looking dashing in his white tie and tails, to his sister. "And here is the princess's escort, Sir Graham Ogden."

Graham bowed gallantly to Heather, and she curtsied.

"I never saw a princess curtsy before," Brian teased.

Graham overheard and winked at Heather. "There never was a princess like this before."

The show ended, and Graham took her to their waiting "coach"—Mr. Ogden's beat-up car. But to Heather, it was every bit as elegant as one in a fairy tale. As for the British diplomat's dress, though he looked quite charming, he had still neglected to comb his hair! Outward appearances meant little to Mr. Ogden. *I like how unpretentious he is,* Heather thought.

At the glamorous King David Hotel, Graham's father pulled up behind a limousine to wait for valet parking. Then an expensive sports car eased behind them. When it was their turn, a footman in uniform opened the door, and Heather swung her legs out gracefully.

Inside Graham checked her stole. Then the three of them got into the receiving line to meet the Israeli President.

"What do I say?" Heather whispered. She'd never been one for formality and was beginning to feel a little nervous about this refined party.

"My father will introduce you," Graham instructed. "The President will say 'It's nice to meet you,' and you say something pleasant in response. That's all! I'm sure you'll do fine."

In fact Heather did quite well and enjoyed meeting the President and his wife. Then they found their table, which was next to the dance floor.

This is great! she thought. *Now I can find Mr. Gilbert and keep an eye on him.*

Although she intended to enjoy Graham's company, she also wanted to learn more about the French diplomat. *He might just be the key person in this case,* she mused.

Although Heather failed to locate him in the large crowd, she did spot Edith Trottier. Her escort looked familiar. The pretty teenager nudged Graham and indicated the couple with a nod. "I'll bet he's the guy from Bethlehem and Nazareth!" she whispered in excitement.

"You may be right," Graham remarked. Then he added, "I still haven't seen Mr. Gilbert."

But Heather temporarily laid aside the mystery when elegant waiters served dinner. She enjoyed the cream of watercress soup, roast leg of lamb with tarragon sauce, parslied rice and buttered asparagus spears. Dessert was hazelnut ice cream with chocolate sauce.

Then she and Graham danced. His father broke in ten minutes later and turned out to be an excellent partner. Heather was much more surprised when Francois Gilbert politely tapped him on the right shoulder.

"May I?" he asked with a nod and a bow.

"Francois!" Nigel Ogden bellowed. "Certainly!"

Heather was thrilled. *What a great way to spy on someone!* she thought with amusement.

"Are you enjoying yourself?" the Frenchman asked.

"Very much. This has been a wonderful evening," she replied. Then asked, "Are you?"

"Uh, yes, of course. I find this relaxing."

"I'm glad," Heather told him. "It seems you've had a rough time recently." She didn't know how much he would tell her, but she figured her probing was worth a try.

"May I ask, what was your grandfather like?" she questioned.

The good-looking diplomat seemed a bit startled. He thought for a moment then replied, "He was formal, honorable, and kind in his way."

Heather tried again. "You seem to have been close."

He laughed a little nervously and cleared his throat. "Uh, yes, we were."

Then he abruptly changed the subject. Heather realized she would learn no more that night. At least not from him.

After they danced another time, Heather excused herself and went upstairs to the restroom. She was about to sit at a vanity to freshen her makeup and hair when she spotted Edith Trottier and several other party-goers come through the door. The teenager lowered her head, hoping Edith had not seen her.

When she passed, Heather quickly got up and slipped into what Israelis called the "water closet." Heather looked through a crack in the door as Edith washed and dried her hands. Then while the Frenchwoman reapplied lipstick, Heather saw a thick wad of paper slip from her purse and fall to the floor. But neither Edith nor anyone else noticed.

After the woman left the room, Heather cautiously went over to pick up the documents. *What a strange thing to carry in an evening purse!* she thought. Then she realized, *These might help me solve the mystery!*

13

Clues from an Ancient Diary

Heather had a quick decision to make. *Edith Trottier could come back for these at any minute,* she considered. *And if she sees me in here, I'm in big trouble.*

She quickly stuffed the papers into her small clutch purse. *I'll go back to the water closet and wait five minutes so we don't run into each other.*

Several other ladies came and went, but Mr. Gilbert's secretary did not. Heather finally left—trying to look like nothing more important than her hair was on her mind.

The young sleuth returned to the ballroom by way of a back staircase rather than the main one or the elevator. *If she suddenly discovers her loss, I don't want to be in her flight path,* she reasoned.

When she arrived at the table, Heather was taken completely by surprise. Graham and his dad were talking to Francois Gilbert, Edith Trottier, and her date! The men stood as she approached.

"I was beginning to think you'd rented the ladies room," Graham joked.

Edith shot a dubious look at Heather, and the teen-ager closed her eyes in a gesture of surrender. *When Edith realizes we were in there together and that those papers are missing . . .* she thought helplessly. Graham noticed Heather's expression but had no idea what he had said wrong.

"Miss Reed, I believe you know my secretary, Edith Trottier," Francois Gilbert said in his courtly manner. "Yes," Heather replied, recovering her poise.

"And this is Paul Flavell, an interpreter at the French consulate," he continued. "Mr. Flavell, Miss Reed." They nodded at each other with forced politeness. "She's visiting from the United States," Gilbert added.

Is this my mysterious Frenchman? Heather wondered as they were seated. *He's certainly arrogant-looking!* Then she glanced at his hands—he was wearing a signet ring with the letter "F!" In addition his voice matched that of the thief from Bethlehem and Nazareth. Heather's eyes caught Graham's. *He knows, too!* she thought with excitement.

"How long will you be staying in Israel?" the haughty Flavell asked. She was sure he asked more out of curiosity than politeness.

"A few more days," she said. *Make him guess,* she thought shrewdly.

"I see," he replied. "I hope your stay will be memorable."

Heather was sure the look that passed between them was a sneer. She almost burst with excitement but kept outwardly calm as the conversation centered on the weather and the President's health.

Then Edith Trottier opened her handbag. *Here it comes!* Heather thought. An expression of horror filled the woman's eyes. Then she stared hard at the American youth.

"Is something wrong?" Heather asked coyly.

Edith swallowed hard. "I seem to have lost my address book."

Now it was Flavell's turn to get jittery. "Are you certain?"

"Yes, I'm certain," she snarled through a phony smile. She turned her poisonous gaze on Heather. The secretary rose from the table, and so did the men. "If you will excuse me, I must find that book. Good evening."

"I will go with you," Flavell stated. "It was nice meeting you, Miss Reed. Perhaps I will see you again."

She nodded and thought, *I wouldn't doubt it.*

Flavell regarded Francois Gilbert sternly, then he and Edith departed in a rush. The puzzled Gilbert said he needed to go as well.

Heather thought, *Whatever show is playing with these people, Mr. Gilbert isn't directing it. He hasn't the faintest idea what's going on.*

She watched the three fade into the crowd. Although Heather was dying to read the papers she had found, she decided to play it safe and wait until the Frenchmen left the hotel.

In the meantime she patiently waited for a chance to tell Graham what was going on. At last they got up to dance again, and she explained to him what had happened in the ladies' room.

"I wish I hadn't opened my big mouth," he moaned.

"You had no way of knowing what had happened," Heather reassured. "Graham, did you see Mr. Flavell's ring?"

"Yes! He's our man, isn't he?"

"Uh-huh. And I'm dying to read those papers Edith dropped!" she added.

It seemed ages before Heather spotted the French trio arguing with each other as they descended the massive staircase. No doubt Edith Trottier had combed the restroom looking for her "address book" and reported the loss. When it didn't turn up following a lengthy search, she and her friends left in a state of alarm. At least that's what Heather figured.

"What's on your mind?" her date asked.

"Those three are working together," she responded. "But I'm still uncertain about Mr. Gilbert's role. Do you think we could leave soon Graham? I have a feeling the papers will tell us what they're up to!"

"Let's find my father after this dance. I'll tell him it's important that we leave."

Nigel Ogden was at the table talking to an engaging—and pretty—Australian diplomat. *This could take forever!* Heather moaned silently as he introduced them.

An hour and a half later they left the hotel. As soon as they got into the battered car, Graham told his father what had happened.

"Let's go straight to the apartment and look at this," Mr. Ogden suggested.

They sat in the living room and eagerly examined the papers, which were photocopies of something handwritten in French.

"I speak some French," Heather announced modestly. Actually, Mr. Ogden's French was quite good. "This could still take time," he said. "The writing is cramped and, well, old."

"Old?" Heather repeated.

"The words are stiff. They're like the French version of King James English."

After fifteen minutes of examining the documents, Heather became excited. "I think these papers were copied from that book you found, Graham!"

"Because the writing is old-fashioned?" he asked eagerly.

"Yes, and because the copy machine picked up some fragments of what looks like pieces of leather," she explained.

Nigel Ogden examined the copies to see for himself. "You are amazing, Heather!"

"Thank you," she said sincerely. "Tell me, have you ever seen that book before, Mr. Ogden?"

"No, I haven't. I've been thinking he might have brought it back from Paris after his grandfather's funeral."

"What does it say?" Graham asked impatiently.

"It seems like the diary of a knight," his father answered. "There's a lot of stuff in here about battles with Moslems."

"Sounds like the Crusades," Graham suggested.

"Yes, it does. He's clearly far from home. Listen to this: 'We journeyed far to that natal locale. We newly wise men.'"

Suddenly it was like a light exploded, shedding its truth in Heather's and Graham's minds. Both said with one voice, "Bethlehem!"

"Read on," they urged.

Mr. Ogden took several minutes to decipher the next passage. "He talks about seeing Bethlehem in the snow! And then, 'Its glorious appearing will come then go as the snow lying thick on Mount with Dome.'"

"That sounds like the snow we just had!" Graham exclaimed.

His father added, "And the references to Mount and Dome could refer to the Dome of the Rock on the Temple Mount!"

Heather gave a start when she looked at the mantel clock. "It's nearly one-thirty! I know Dr. Samra will be waiting up. I'd better call."

The sleepy professor gave Heather permission to stay an hour longer. The three went straight back to work.

Several minutes later Graham squealed like a little boy. "You'll never believe this!" Heather and his dad dropped what they were doing and crowded around him. "Look at these drawings!" He pointed to faded images, one inside the other.

"That one looks like a church." Mr. Ogden pointed to the outside one.

Heather agreed. "It looks an awful lot like St. Anne's." When she realized what she had said, she gave a start. "St. Anne's!"

"Look closer," Graham urged. "What's inside?"

She put the page directly under a lamp. "It looks like a cup." Several seconds later Heather cried out, "The Grail!"

14

Secret of St. Anne's Church

So that's what this is all about!" Mr. Ogden exclaimed. "The Holy Grail." He whistled long and low. "But how in the world did Francois acquire this book?"

"He probably did get it in France," Heather remarked. "That is, if you've never seen it on his desk before, and he's acted strangely since he came back."

They were quiet for some moments, each alone with his thoughts. Then Heather broke the stillness.

"This French knight believed the Grail would reappear at a certain time. And it seems like this is it—there's snow on the Dome of the Rock. These papers show the Grail would appear in each place where there have recently been incidents, beginning in Bethlehem." She picked up a paper and read aloud, "'Lastly unto the least of these, a visitation to the mother of our Blessed Virgin. Then, the times shall end—and no more.'"

Mr. Ogden said, "The 'mother of our Blessed Virgin' would be St. Anne!"

Heather became even more excited. "St. Anne's will be the last place the Grail appears! But I don't quite understand that. How can it just show up in one place, then disappear?"

"In the legends the Grail has miraculous powers, including the ability to come and go," Graham explained.

"But that's impossible," Heather protested.

"Regardless, that's what the stories say."

She sank back on the couch. "I'm certain Edith Trottier and Paul Flavell have been stalking the Grail and trying to scare me away. But I still don't understand why Mr. Gilbert tried getting into the Garden Tomb. Do you know about that, Mr. Ogden?"

"Yes. Graham told me. But I find it hard to believe of Francois." He paused then added, "I'll speak with him after church tomorrow."

"And we can go to St. Anne's to investigate," Graham suggested.

"Not alone," his father forbade. "That's a dangerous part of the city. I'll take you."

Heather felt relieved. *It isn't just the locals who worry me,* she thought darkly. *This French duo might stop at nothing to get the Grail—including murder!*

When the teenager got back to her room that night, she locked the photocopies in her suitcase. "I'll put them in a safe-deposit box at the front desk tomorrow," she decided. In spite of her exhilaration over her fairy-tale evening at the diplomats' ball and the latest developments in the mystery, Heather fell right to sleep.

The following day the Ogdens picked up Heather after church and the noon meal. Graham's dad had exciting news. "I spoke to a White Father this morning and arranged an interview with him at St. Anne's. We're to meet him at the side entrance near the pool."

"That's wonderful!" she exclaimed.

"Well, you kids have got me interested in this, too. Besides," he added, "it involves my friend."

Moments later Mr. Ogden parked across from the gate to the old city wall. As they walked in the brisk afternoon air, Heather noted aloud, "The snow's melting. The Grail hunters don't have much time."

At St. Anne's the British diplomat rang a bell at the side entrance. A short, middle-aged priest wearing a white robe answered. "Hello, I'm Father André," he welcomed them. "You must be the Ogdens." He had a pleasant French accent.

"That's correct," Nigel said. "And this is our friend, Heather Reed."

It's the same priest who told our group we couldn't go inside! Heather thought.

"Please come in." The priest led them to a modestly furnished parlor. "I understand you have some questions about our church?"

"I'm especially interested in what made the Moslem authorities give St. Anne's to the French government," Heather began, thinking of the information Francois Gilbert had given her about the church's history.

The friendly cleric suddenly looked nervous. "That part is somewhat confusing," he answered vaguely.

But she wouldn't give up. "Tell us what you know then." When he still hesitated, she became more determined to get an answer. "Is it a secret?"

"No, Miss Reed, it is not," he replied. "But it is fanciful." He tried to look haughty about it.

"Sounds interesting," she pursued.

"I suppose," he sighed, looking like he suddenly regretted giving the interview. Finally he admitted, "The Moslems didn't want St. Anne's because they heard strange cries here and believed it was haunted."

"Haunted!" Nigel Ogden expressed.

"Thought to be," he corrected, raising his index finger. "The church is known for its sustained echo. I am certain there was a logical reason for anything they heard."

When he fell silent, Heather begged, "Oh, please tell us more!" She was filled with excitement. And to herself, she thought, *Maybe there's a connection between the Crusader's echo and the one I heard the other day!*

Father André coughed. "Very well. Back in the twelfth century the Christians were driven out of Jerusalem by the Moslem leader Saladin. One French knight bravely tried to defeat Saladin's men single-handedly after his companions fled."

"What happened to him?" Heather asked, sitting on the edge of her seat.

"He hid in an underground vault," the priest said. "But he was discovered, and Saladin's men sealed him inside."

"That's monstrous!" Mr. Ogden cried out.

"Would you show us the vault?" Heather requested, thinking it might have a connection to the present mystery.

Father André found himself taking his visitors to the church's underbelly. But he carefully avoided the sanctuary where Heather had heard the frightening echo. "There is a beautiful wall mosaic marking the spot," he said.

Heather admired the scene that showed the knight looking peaceful in death as his enemies raged outside his tomb. Upon closer examination, the teenager discovered a fascinating detail. In the upper part of the mosaic angels sang. And in the midst of them a golden cup glowed. *The Grail!* Heather thought excitedly. She pointed it out to the others when Father André looked away.

When they were about to end the tour, the French priest took them aside. "I have heard the echo myself just this week," he admitted in a whisper.

"Is that why the church is closed?" Heather asked, wondering when the weird noises began.

He nodded. "And there have been signs of digging below. I have even found the remains of a meal."

I'll bet Edith Trottier and Paul Flavell are behind this, she thought. Then Heather asked, "Have you called the police?"

"We have contacted our authority, which is the French Consulate," he told her.

Which means nothing is being done about it, Heather thought grimly. A glance at her British friends told her they were thinking the same thing.

"Do you know something about this?" asked Father André with a worried gaze.

Nigel Ogden looked first at Heather, then at his son. Each silently communicated his willingness to let the priest in on the mystery. Then the big Englishman said, "Yes, Father, we do. But you must consider this information as secret as what you would be told in confession."

"I will," the distressed Father André agreed soberly. "But I would feel better hearing this upstairs."

Thirty minutes later, after securing the priest's promise to keep them informed of further developments, the Ogdens and Heather left. In the car Mr. Ogden made an announcement. "I'm going to pay Francois a visit," he said. "We need to solve this crazy puzzle before someone gets hurt."

"I'm sure Edith Trottier and Paul Flavell are causing that weird echo at St. Anne's," Heather added. "But I still can't quite figure out how Mr. Gilbert fits in."

"And because they're in authority, nothing has been done to stop them," Graham stated.

"At least nothing official." Heather smiled slyly.

Mr. Ogden dropped the teenagers off at a coffee shop, desiring to speak with Francois alone. Heather and Graham discussed their visit to St. Anne's over steaming cups of tea, then went for a walk. Again it seemed they were being followed.

"Maybe we're a bit jittery," Graham concluded.

"We have reason to be."

Just then a man leading a camel bounded up to the couple imploring them to ride his animal. At first they ignored him, but he persisted.

"You cannot visit Jerusalem without a camel ride," he urged. "Only five American dollars!" The animal's lazy eyes regarded them indifferently.

Graham paused. "I suppose he's right, Heather. It's really quite an experience."

"I'm sure it is!" she laughed.

"One you will never forget," the pushy man asserted.

"My treat," Graham offered. "But I won't pay more than three dollars," he told the owner.

They bartered, and the English teenager won out. Then the man assisted Heather onto the awkward camel's humped back. She disliked the way it pitched forward to rise.

"This is so weird," she said nervously.

"It's okay," Graham assured her. "They do that."

But this time the camel didn't do it right. With a sudden jerking motion, it sent Heather tumbling right over its head!

15

Desperate Measures

Heather landed on her knees, and scraped her hands trying to soften the fall. Graham dashed to her side and gently pushed her out of the beast's way. The camel's owner just stood there with a funny look on his face.

"Are you all right?" the British teenager asked, his voice full of concern.

"I think so," she said quietly.

Graham called attention to the palms of her hands and her right knee. They were scratched and bleeding. Then he shouted at the man, "What is this all about?"

The man pulled the camel out of the way, making a great fuss. "This has never happened before," he maintained.

The young man's eyes blazed. "Then why now?"

"If I tell you, will you not report me?" the man pleaded.

Graham's temper was getting hot, and Heather spoke up. "We won't report you if you tell us." Even in her pain she grew excited thinking they might pick up another clue.

"A woman paid me to do that," he charged. "But she wanted you hurt badly. I only let my camel frighten you."

"What do you call those scratches?" Graham yelled.

"What did she look like?" Heather queried.

"Young and mean," the toothless man said.

"Edith Trottier," Graham remarked sourly. Heather exhaled deeply.

The camel man quickly summoned a taxi for them and insisted he pay the fare to Graham's home. Heather wanted to wash up there to avoid her brother's probing questions. Mrs. Bursa, the Ogdens' housekeeper, cleaned Heather's wounds as she muttered under her breath about careless camel drivers. Mr. Ogden returned shortly afterward and listened to the story. He was deeply upset.

"I'm glad you're all right, Heather," he said. "But this may be getting too risky to continue."

"We're getting so close!" she contended.

"Precisely why it's so unsafe," he insisted. He looked down at his feet and sighed heavily.

"What's wrong, Dad?" Graham asked.

"I can't find Francois."

"Can't find him?" he repeated.

He shook his head. "He wasn't in his apartment. His neighbors told me they never heard him come home last night and he's not been there all day."

"Maybe he went somewhere after the ball," Heather suggested.

"I thought of that, too," the diplomat said. "But at the ball I asked him to come home with us. I thought it might help you to talk with him again. He claimed he was tired and would be going straight to his apartment."

"Let's look for him," she proposed.

"I'm taking you right back to the kibbutz," Mr. Ogden said firmly. "You had a bad experience today."

There was no changing his mind. Heather returned to the hotel realizing just how tired and sore she felt. After dinner the teenager slept for ten hours.

Following a lecture with an Israeli professor the next morning, the Kirby College students toured the splendid Israel Museum. They returned to the kibbutz at two o'clock.

When Heather and Michelle opened the door to their room, they gasped. Someone had forced open their suitcases and dumped their contents all over the room. The beds were stripped and slashed. On the bathroom mirror was a skull and crossbones in lipstick.

Michelle called the manager, and the room quickly filled with students, kibbutz management, and police. The young ladies answered questions, then got moved to another room.

When they got settled, Michelle went swimming with Tony. Heather welcomed the privacy and called Graham about the break-in. He blamed himself. "If I hadn't opened my big mouth, Edith Trottier wouldn't have suspected you had her missing papers."

"Please don't blame yourself," she comforted him. "Besides they didn't find those diary entries. They're in a safe-deposit box."

Graham praised her cleverness, then said he had news about Francois Gilbert. "My father visited his office, but he wasn't there. Edith said he'd gone to Tel Aviv, but Dad sensed she was lying. When he left the building, he saw her go out the back entrance and drive away."

"I'm afraid Mr. Gilbert is in danger," Heather said.

"It looks that way, doesn't it?" Graham agreed.

"I want to reread those papers," she said. "We really didn't have time to be thorough the other night."

When she hung up, Heather got the photocopies and poured over them for the next three hours. Though she still couldn't find the writer's name, the amateur detective learned he was a Knight Templar. She remembered that most of those knights had been French and guarded pilgrims to the Holy Land during the Crusades. Heather assumed a reference to Haifa meant the knight was writing from that port city.

With growing excitement she discovered this warrior had been among those who had escaped from St. Anne's during Saladin's siege! And she noticed more details concerning the Grail's reappearance, including this entry: "Should a trespasser trespass against us, let him be as the brave, doomed Knight sealed in his Crusading crypt!"

The teenager felt chills run up her spine. And there was another astonishing item: "When the Wise Man comes on appointed day, the Cup will await where it all began. Then no more until His new Coming."

Heather lay back against a pillow. *The Wise Men again,* she reflected, winding a piece of hair around her finger. *But they've already searched for the Grail in Bethlehem.* Just then a casual look at Michelle's open date book provided the key to unlock the mystery! It was the sixth of January. In small letters under the date it said, "Epiphany."

Her mind kicked into high gear as the items came together all at once. *Epiphany marks the appearance of the Wise Men in Bethlehem to honor the baby Jesus,* she considered. *And it's the last day the Grail will appear, according to this diary. Maybe Mr. Gilbert tried to stop Edith and Paul from finding it. He may be in danger!*

Heather placed an urgent call to Graham. "Can you meet me at St. Anne's as soon as possible?" She quickly filled him in.

"That's amazing!" he exclaimed. "I'll be there right away."

"Can your dad come?"

"No. He's at a meeting," Graham said.

Heather left a note for Dr. Samra under his door saying she'd be at St. Anne's with her English friend.

The teenagers met at the church and stealthily made their way inside. Even so, the terrible echo "caught" them. "Turn back or die!" bounced ominously off the church's walls.

"We must stop it!" Heather cried. "Or we'll give ourselves away."

"I think it's a recording that gets activated when we cross a light beam," Graham whispered. He promptly located its source. "Here it is!" He pointed out a device in the back of the sanctuary. Within moments he had deactivated the "ghost."

Then Graham and Heather proceeded slowly down a side staircase. "I hear digging," Heather whispered.

"Me, too," her friend stated.

But they had no opportunity to track it down. When they reached the bottom, a knight in armor lunged at the horrified teenagers with a long, deadly sword!

Graham grabbed Heather's arm and pulled her away in the nick of time!

Then the menacing knight lifted the weapon for another murderous strike! Although his movements were clunky, the sword gave him the advantage.

"Look!" Heather cried out, spotting another door.

They made a run for it, barely outdistancing the knight. They found themselves outside next to the Pool of Bethesda and sprinted through the ruins, looking for a hiding place. Heather moved faster than she dreamed possible through the ancient stone porches. *God, please help us,* she prayed.

Through the arches and across the bridges they ran in what seemed like a hopeless game of hide-and-seek. Then just when the young people thought they were safe at last, the knight emerged from behind a stone wall. There was nowhere to go now but the dark cavern looming behind them. They stood still and faced their cruel enemy.

Fear paralyzed Heather as she watched the knight lift his huge sword with an evil laugh. As the weapon descended, Graham forcefully pushed her into the dark abyss.

16

Buried Alive!

Heather was too stunned to think. She fell helplessly in the darkness then hit the water with a sudden jolt. When she stopped plunging downward, she propelled herself up with her legs and arms. The young woman broke the surface and opened her eyes, but it was too dark to see. *Not again!* she groaned, thinking of the water tunnel ordeal.

"Heather!" Graham whispered loudly. "Are you okay?"

"Yes," she responded, treading water. "You made a smart move. Where is our friend now?"

Guided by the sound of Heather's voice, Graham moved toward her. "I believe he's gone, thank God. I don't think he'll come in after us. That armor would send him straight to the bottom."

"I see light at the opening now," Heather announced as her eyes adjusted to the murkiness. "When my group was here earlier, we discovered there's only a rock wall behind us. Our only way out is to climb to the ledge we jumped off and hope the knight really is gone."

It took the teenagers fifteen minutes to scale the slick wall separating the water from the ledge. They used its slimy stones as footholds, which proved tricky with their wet shoes.

At last Graham boosted himself over the edge. Then he pulled Heather to safety. The young people warily looked around for their attacker, but he had gone.

"Who do you think that was?" Graham asked, rubbing water out of his hair.

Heather grimaced. "Paul Flavell, since we only know of three suspects. I doubt Mr. Gilbert would try to hurt us." She emptied her sneakers with a sigh. "Cold feet again!"

Her friend added, "Edith is too small for that armor."

"Graham, I feel nervous about that digging sound we heard in the church."

"Me, too," he agreed.

"We've got to go back," Heather insisted. "Mr. Gilbert probably tried to stop them. If they're picking up their cues from that diary, they may bury him alive for interfering!"

"You're much braver than I, but I'll follow!" he pledged.

They headed cautiously back to the church. "Does your dad know where you are?" Heather asked. Graham shook his head. "Then we can't count on outside help. I left a message for Dr. Samra, but who knows when he'll get it. Maybe a priest will hear us." She concluded, "If not, we'll have to outsmart them."

The teenagers cautiously reentered the lower level of St. Anne's. Heather saw light pouring from a deep but open vault. "Look!" she whispered.

Her friend turned in that direction. "And I hear that digging again," he remarked.

Instantly they heard another, chilling sound—a man's muffled cries. But it came from the opposite direction!

Graham leaned close to Heather. "Mr. Gilbert?"

"I'd say so," she replied grimly.

They followed the distressed sobs to a far corner of the underground room. "Look, Graham!" Heather pointed. "This is the mosaic of the French knight who was buried alive!"

Next to it was a sealed grave in the wall. The teenagers ran their hands across the vault but quickly pulled back.

"I feel fresh cement!" Graham announced. "I'll bet Francois Gilbert is in there!"

"We must work fast," Heather urged. "We'll get you out!" she shouted softly at the wall. The muted response encouraged them.

They dug at the wall with Graham's pocket knife for what seemed an eternity. Even as they made progress, the noises in the other part of the basement went on uninterrupted. It was beyond them why the criminals didn't try to stop them. But they didn't have time to think about that now. Freeing the French diplomat was their biggest concern.

"Mr. Gilbert?" Heather called when they got closer. "Is it you?"

A faint yes came through the wall.

"Don't worry! We'll get you out!" Graham encouraged.

But a few minutes later a deep voice startled the couple. "What do you think you're doing?"

The terrified teenagers swung around, ready to die by the sword. Then their faces lit up. "Father André!" they cried out.

"Shh!" he warned. "I heard that echo awhile ago and finally got up enough courage to investigate. What are you doing to the wall?" he challenged. They quickly told him what had happened. Within minutes the priest was helping them break loose wet cement until they reached the vault behind it.

At last their efforts paid off. Graham helped a very stiff and frightened French diplomat out of the crypt.

"How can I ever thank you?" he wept softly.

Heather glanced inside but quickly looked away in disgust. In the crypt was the Knight Templar's skeleton!

Suddenly a cry rang out from the other end of the catacombs. They proceeded cautiously in the direction of the sound and found Edith Trottier and Paul Flavell looking elated. The latter wore black jeans, a sweatshirt—and the armor's breastplate. Unfortunately Francois stumbled and gave the investigators away.

An evil smile spread across Edith Trottier's hard face as she spotted them. "The Holy Grail!" she shouted, triumphantly lifting a gleaming gold cup. "Not even you stopped us," she hissed at Heather. "We will live forever, but you have only a few more minutes!"

Paul Flavell grabbed the knight's deadly sword. "All of you, back in the crypt!" he ordered. "Go join the heroic Knight Templar!" He laughed wickedly.

This was too much for Francois Gilbert, and he passed out. Father André caught him.

As they moved under sword-point toward the dreaded grave, dragging Mr. Gilbert along, the trio heard a thunderous noise. In seconds Mr. Ogden and Dr. Samra burst into the room with several guards from the French Consulate.

The startled Edith Trottier dropped the precious cup. To everyone's amazement, it shattered into a hundred pieces! The Grail had been a fake! All their efforts had been futile.

Edith lunged at Heather in her anger and despair, but a guard separated them. Mr. Ogden quickly shielded the American girl. In seconds Trottier and her accomplice were led away in handcuffs.

Later that afternoon Heather, Graham and his dad, Dr. Samra, Francois Gilbert, and Father André gathered in the Ogdens' living room. The housekeeper brought them hot tea and cakes as they discussed the mystery.

"This morning's mail contained a note from Francois asking for help," Mr. Ogden recounted. "Then Dr. Samra called and told me Heather and Graham had gone to St. Anne's. I picked him up at the kibbutz and headed straight to the French Consulate for help."

"You showed up in the nick of time!" Heather praised them. "It was just like a movie ending." She paused, then asked the French diplomat, "I still haven't figured out how you got that knight's diary."

The handsome man was beginning to return to his normal self after his brush with death. "After my grandfather's funeral in Paris, my grandmother gave me that old diary," Gilbert told Heather. "Its author was Francois of Clairveaux, a Knight Templar in the Crusades and my ancestor."

"Is that right?" a surprised Nigel Ogden exclaimed.

"Yes. You see right before my grandfather died, a French museum curator found the book in an old depository. He recognized our family crest on the inside and presented it to my grandfather. The pages had been bound by another relative in the eighteenth century. When Grandfather realized it contained information about the Holy Grail, he wanted me to know about it. He'd always been interested in the Grail legend and planned to go over the diary's mysterious instructions with me. But he died a few days later."

Francois sighed and hung his head. "I wanted to find the Grail and present it to the French government in my family's name. I never desired the wealth or immortality it is said to bring." A sob caught in his throat. "Now I have disgraced my family."

Nigel Ogden put an arm around his shoulders. "You've done no such thing," he comforted. "I think you acted nobly." Father André assured Gilbert that he would tell the priests at the Garden Tomb what had really happened.

"I'll bet Edith Trottier and Paul Flavell ruined your plans," Heather guessed. "But how?"

"You are very clever," he complimented the teenager. "Edith found the diary on my desk when I was out, and she read it. She was dating Paul Flavell and told him about it. They offered to help me, but I refused. Then Edith said I would have to let them help because they knew the secret, too. She had even made photocopies."

"That's how I figured out what happened to you," Heather explained. She told him about the restroom incident at the ball as well as other clues that helped her along the way, including Flavell's signet ring.

"I am amazed," he admired. "I became deeply distressed when you told me about the water tunnel at Megiddo. I threatened to report Edith and Paul, but I should have simply done it. They said unless I broke into the Garden Tomb, they would kill you, Heather."

"I'm glad I didn't know that!" she exclaimed.

He continued. "As we left the diplomats' ball, Edith said she had lost photocopied pages of the diary. Then they forced me to drive to her apartment at gunpoint. Fortunately I managed to send that distress note to Nigel beforehand. Later they drugged me. Then I woke up in that horrible crypt." He shuddered.

Mr. Ogden said, "And to think that Grail was a fake all along!"

A little smile brightened Francois' expression. "From other accounts of my ancestor's life, he was quite a teller of tales."

The group burst out laughing. Then Heather said,

"It's still a shame the fake Grail was destroyed. It was hundreds of years old." She paused. "But it was worth it just to see that look on Edith's face!"

They all laughed once again. Then Francois surprised Heather when he handed her his ancestor-knight's diary. "I want you to have this as a souvenir," he announced. "Please accept it along with my sincere gratitude for all you did to help me. And may your unusual talents for solving mysterious difficulties enable you to help many others."

Everyone joyfully agreed.

"Promise you will write and tell me about all the new mysteries you solve." Graham took Heather's hand and held it tightly. In a few days they would say good-bye to each other.

Heather's eyes misted. "I promise."

ABOUT THE AUTHOR

Rebecca Price Janney has dual careers as both a writer and a teacher. As a freelance writer, she has had numerous articles published in newspapers and magazines, including *Seventeen, Decision, Moody Monthly, World Vision, Childlife, War Cry,* and *The Young Salvationist.* Her published work also includes a section in *Shaped by God's Love,* an anthology published by World Wide Publishers. As a teacher at Cabrini College, her speciality is Jewish and Middle East History. Rebecca and her husband Scott live in suburban Philadelphia.

Four new, exciting whodunits!

THE HEATHER REED SERIES

It's no mystery why this series is catching on! Heather Reed is a sixteen-year-old with an uncanny ability to be in the right place at the wrong time. Her unquenchable curiosity guarantees suspense-filled, mystery adventures young readers will want to read over and over again.

#1—The Cryptic Clue

When the Reed's next-door neighbor, a famous history professor, mysteriously disappears, Heather is determined to find out what happened, but her curiosity brings her within a heartbeat of tragedy. A hidden clue draws her into the nerve center of a vengeful international plot.

#2—The Model Mystery

Top competitors in The American Model of the Year Contest have received anonymous threats. Heather Reed decides to try her hand at reporting for a popular teenage magazine—what better way to find out why a beauty competition has suddenly turned ugly? But before she can reveal the culprits' prideful plot, Heather and her best friend find themselves in serious danger.

#3—The Eerie Echo

During a student tour to Israel, Heather soon finds out that not everything in the Holy Land is holy. A mystery soon unfolds that involves mysterious catacombs, a haunted church, a missing French ambassador, and a priceless Christian artifact.

#4—The Toxic Secret

When a well-known environmental activist receives death threats and becomes gravely ill, sixteen-year-old amateur detective Heather Reed deciphers the strange and intriguing facts. This suspenseful whodunit combines old-fashioned mystery with issues that are important to today's young readers.